THE OTTER'S WINGS

Also by Mary E. Lowd

The Bee's Waltz
The Snake's Song: A Labyrinth of Souls Novel
Entanglement Bound
    The Entangled Universe, Book 1
The Entropy Fountain
    The Entangled Universe, Book 2
Starwhal in Flight
    The Entangled Universe, Book 3
Tri-Galactic Trek
Nexus Nine
Otters In Space
Otters In Space 2: Jupiter, Deadly
Otters In Space 3: Octopus Ascending
In a Dog's World
When a Cat Loves a Dog
Jove Deadly's Lunar Detective Agency
The Necromouser and Other Magical Cats
Lunar Cavity

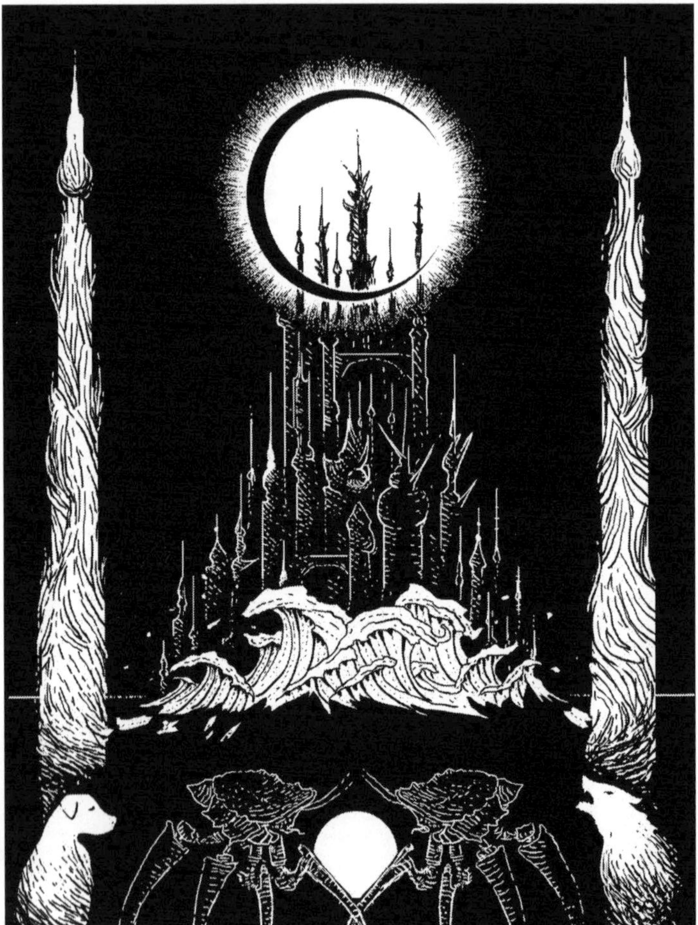

The Otter's Wings

A Labyrinth of Souls Novel

by

Mary E. Lowd

ShadowSpinners Press

Copyright © 2022 Mary E. Lowd

All rights reserved,
including the right to reproduce this book,
or portions thereof, in any form.

Cover art by Josephe Vandel.
Book design by Matthew Lowes.

ShadowSpinners Press
shadowspinnerspress.com

Typeset in
Minion Pro by Robert Slimbach
and IM FELL Double Pica by Igino Marini.
The Fell Types are digitally reproduced
by Igino Marini, www.iginomarini.com.

Learn more about
the Labyrinth of Souls game at
matthewlowes.com/games.

For Quinn

Editor's Preface

Dungeon Solitaire: Labyrinth of Souls is a fantasy game for tarot cards, written by Matthew Lowes and Illustrated by Josephe Vandel. In the game you defeat monsters, disarm traps, open doors, and explore mazes as you delve the depths of a dangerous dungeon. Along the way you collect treasure and magic items, gain skills, and gather companions.

Now ShadowSpinners Press is publishing this and other stand-alone novels inspired by the game. Each *Labyrinth of Souls* novel features a journey into a unique vision of the underworld.

The Labyrinth of Souls is more than an ancient ruin filled with monsters, trapped treasure, and the lost tombs of bygone kings. It is a manifestation of a mythic underworld, existing at a crossroads between people and cultures, between time and space, between the physical world and the deepest reaches of the psyche. It is a dark mirror held up to human experience, in which you may find your dreams … or your doom. Entrances to this realm can appear in any time period, in any location. There are innumerable reasons why a person may enter, but it is a place antagonistic to those who do, a place where monsters dwell, with obstacles and illusions to waylay adventurers, and whose very walls can be a force of corruption. It is a haunted place, ever at the edge of sanity.

The Otter's Wings

The Celestial Fragments

Book Three

1

Witch-Hazel grew up in the countryside where squirrels still built their own nests out of twigs, dried leaves, and bits of grass. She'd never been very good at building nests or finding the stashes of nuts she'd buried in the fall when springtime came.

She'd never felt very good at being a squirrel.

So when she heard a song of the larger world, she'd left her home and gone adventuring. Witch-Hazel's adventures had taken her deep under the Earth, through labyrinths and enchanted groves, and high into the sky where the All-Being's castle floated on an orchard of clouds. She'd seen the length and height of the world, and she'd discovered while she wasn't any good at finding buried stashes of nuts, she was good at finding lost treasures—especially in the form of magical Celestial Fragments and, even better, absent friends.

Yet even through all of her adventures, Witch-Hazel had never seen a place like Riverton.

The animals of Riverton had worked together—otters, beavers, hedgehogs, salamanders, lizards, songbirds, badgers, and more—to build great structures, hewing logs into walls, and arranging walls into cabins. Living thickets of shrubs had been woven together, their branches forming buildings as well. An entire city with cobblestone streets, paved with pebbles worn smooth by the river, stood between the lazy curve of the river and the sheer cliffside of the mountain rising behind it.

After all her travels, Witch-Hazel could hardly believe such a wondrous place existed only a day's journey from her own family's oak grove. Yet through her whole childhood, they'd never thought of coming here. Her life had been a few families of squirrels, friendly with each other but all struggling to get by, building nests and collecting nuts in a single grove of oak trees.

The world had seemed so small when she'd been young, but now she knew, it never had been.

Power flowed through the city of Riverton in the form of water, crashing and splashing, over great wooden wheels. Inside the buildings, there were even greater wonders—electric lights, steam-powered elevators, and music stored on ceramic discs that could be played back at any time. Modern life. Witch-Hazel loved it.

Her companions were less happy.

Fish-Breath and Twiggy had grown up in Riverton, friends from the beginning. The jovial otter and mechanically-minded beaver had left Riverton on a quest, and they'd returned as failures. They hadn't restored the celestial rivers that had flowed from the All-Being's castle

The Otter's Wings

in the sky all the way down to the Earth like godly waterfalls. They had returned as laughing-stocks, fools to have ever believed in those ancient rivers at all.

Of course, Witch-Hazel knew they weren't fools. The three of them had stood in the All-Being's castle together, faced the miraculous and terrifying god, and been told of how the cracks in the Sun, Moon, and North Star were allowing magic to drain from the world, drying up the rivers.

That was why the rivers couldn't be restored. At least, not until the cracks in the celestial bodies had been healed.

But those cracks couldn't be healed without the Celestial Fragments embedded in Fish-Breath's body—three sparkling gemstones were keeping the jolly otter alive, granting him the magical powers of strength, flight, and endless breath that had saved him from dying, brave and martyred, while fighting zombies until his final breath.

They'd been through a lot, the three of them.

But they'd returned to Riverton not as heroes, but as laughable clowns. Witch-Hazel didn't mind. She'd always been seen as a fool, and she'd never been to Riverton before; she didn't know the animals there; and she wouldn't have believed her own stories if she hadn't lived through them herself. They sounded like tall tales.

Fish-Breath though turned further and further inward, keeping his majestic wings—the boon granted by the gleaming Star Sliver, embedded in the flesh and fur of his wrist—folded tightly against his back. Most of the time, he draped a cloak over himself, woven from a simple cloth, a similar tawny shade to the feathered wings underneath. It tore him apart every time a Riverton resident laughed at his wings, calling them fake, instead of at his jokes and intentional buffoonery.

He wanted to tell tall tales. Not be one.

Besides, the wings were part of him now. A part he wasn't sure he wanted … but a part of him, no less.

Twiggy took the mockery even harder, since most of the animals of Riverton assumed the wings, which they believed to be fake, were something she'd constructed. A mechanical trick, worn over Fish-Breath's back, held onto him with hidden straps.

Twiggy hated being complimented for building something she hadn't. In her time, she'd invented many things—mechanical torches, improvised boats and trampolines, and even a hot air balloon. None of them were jokes. None of them were tricks. For all that the beaver loved her jocular friend Fish-Breath, she was not a joker. Deep down, she was a very serious being, and it killed her inside to see everyone she'd ever known—all the animals she'd grown up with, people who'd known her for her whole life—misunderstand her so deeply that they'd think she was lying and had built a useless pair of wings for show.

Twiggy's inventions were useful. And she would never lie about them.

The Otter's Wings

Of course, Fish-Breath's wings weren't useless. He could fly with them. But after the reception he'd received from his old friends and family, he didn't want to share that part of himself with them. He didn't want to prove himself.

So, Fish-Breath, Twiggy, and Witch-Hazel lived uncomfortably in Riverton—the squirrel enjoying the new sights to see, while the otter and beaver shirked and shied away from their role as sights themselves.

Witch-Hazel hoped and assumed her friends would adjust to the situation over time. This was their home, after all, and she hoped to make it hers too. Their disappointment at returning home as a laughingstock instead of as legendary heroes would fade. The strangeness of Fish-Breath's wings would be forgotten as people slowly realized he wasn't going to suddenly stop sporting them, and Twiggy would busy herself with new inventions for which she'd gain properly earned accolades.

All would be well. And Fish-Breath could carry the three gemstones, the Celestial Fragments, as part of his body for the rest of his—hopefully very long—life with Witch-Hazel in Riverton. Someday, after he had passed from this life, the Celestial Fragments could be returned to the cracks in the Sun, Moon, and Northern Star. For now, the good otter would simply borrow them. He was very deserving, and his life, no matter how long it seemed to Witch-Hazel, would be short on a Celestial scale.

The Sun, the Moon, and the Northern Star could wait. She could see them in the sky, as she walked, side by side with Fish-Breath toward his favorite tavern. The golden edge of the sun slipped under the horizon, leaving a hazy glow behind, silhouetting all the buildings; the moon rose like a silver plate, cool and bright; and the Northern Star was the first twinkling glimmer of starlight to pierce the fading twilight of the sky. They were ageless compared to mortal beings.

Celestial bodies could wait; Witch-Hazel's gurgling belly could not. She'd spent the day with Fish-Breath, down by the side of the river, learning to fish with poles Twiggy had built them, complete with hooks and lines. Fish-Breath was a fish-whisperer, and while Witch-Hazel hadn't caught a single fish under his tutelage, he'd lured several dozen onto his own line. The slippery, silvery, dripping morsels hung over his back, still strung on their lines, like a strange, soggy, scaly, stinky bouquet.

When they got to the tavern, Fish-Breath wielded the bundle of fingerling fish like a trophy and bartered them to the barkeep for meals and drinks for himself, Witch-Hazel, and Twiggy for the next two days.

They spent the evening in Witch-Hazel's favorite way—drinking peach cider, munching on toasted nuts, and gabbing with the other patrons of the bar. Witch-Hazel didn't say much herself, but she loved listening to Fish-Breath and some of the rabbits who also ate at the bar nightly try to top each other's tall tales. She and Twiggy usually played a few rounds of the various bar games—tossing acorns at a cauldron; carefully removing twigs from a tower; or building houses of leaves, while holding their breaths so as not to knock the delicate structures down with a careless exhalation.

Twiggy was a master of leaf buildings, creating complicated castles from nothing but delicate, dried detritus. Witch-Hazel was getting quite good at tossing acorns, and while she was clumsy about building her own leaf buildings, she considered it a win if she simply didn't knock down one of Twiggy's leaf castles. The withering gaze she earned from the beaver if she did laugh too uproariously at one of Fish-Breath's jokes—sending an hour's work flying like so much autumn breeze—was enough to chill the merriest of hearts.

Tonight though, Twiggy was running late, and Witch-Hazel found herself at loose ends while Fish-Breath told the story of their adventures—culminating with their escape from the All-Being's castle—yet another time, having discovered a fresh set of ears. This time the otter's audience was a hedgehog, traveling through town, and decorated with colorful flower petals speared on most of his prickly spines. He had a lovely sense of fashion but otherwise seemed a rather dull fellow and was utterly entranced by Fish-Breath's stories.

Witch-Hazel found herself getting caught up in the story as well.

"These sorcerer crabs surrounded us!" Fish-Breath exclaimed. "Waving and clacking their claws, like they meant to cut our heads right off with them, and suddenly—WHOOSH!" Fish-Breath waved his paws in a wild imitation of the waterworks the crabs had weaponized against him, Witch-Hazel, and Twiggy. "Threads and ropes of water! Everywhere! Hitting us as hard as actual whips! Why, I was flabbergasted. Here these crabs were supposed to be the guardians of the eternal river, and they'd clearly gone mad in that cave deep underground, attacking harmless pilgrims like us. I could hardly think with all the water slapping me in the face."

This was the part of the story where Witch-Hazel always started to feel self-conscious when she remembered it for herself. But somehow, when Fish-Breath told it, everything went differently.

"Then Witch-Hazel whipped out this ancient sword she'd found in a mole city and WHACK, WHICK, WHOCK!"

The hedgehog's eyes widened. "What happened?" he asked breathlessly, hanging on Fish-Breath's every word.

Fish-Breath leaned back, crossing his arms across his chest, milking the moment for all it was worth. "Well, Twiggy and I are water mammals, so you'd think we'd have kept our heads about us, even with those supernatural

The Otter's Wings

ropes of water slapping across our faces, but no, we were just too shocked to think straight. But this little squirrel, who I'd thought was tagging along and needed MY protection, showed herself for the hero she is: she chopped those maniacal, crazed crab's eyestalks right off, clearing the path for us to get away. I couldn't believe how quickly she got her paws under her and swung that sword, protecting us. Just a little squirrel with a sword almost too big to hold without falling over backwards, and she saved us all from SORCERERS who were trying to kill us. I could hardly believe it."

Witch-Hazel could hardly believe it herself, and she'd been there. At the time, she'd been scared, uncertain, and as soon as the sword was swinging, terrified she'd blinded those sorcerer crabs for no reason. That she was the true villain in the story. But Fish-Breath never wavered in his version: she was a hero. She loved him for that.

The otter went on with his story, completely in his element. He was so delighted to have found someone who didn't think him a fraud that at the end of the long story, Fish-Breath pulled the rough hewn cloak off his back and spread the tawny wings he'd been gifted by the Celestial Fragments. "See?" Fish-Breath flapped his wings gently, careful not to disturb any of the other patrons in the crowded bar.

The hedgehog laughed, a full-on guffaw from deep in his belly, and Witch-Hazel, who hadn't expected this turn of events, looked about the bar hurriedly, hoping no one else was paying attention. But they were.

Chuckles rippled among the groups of rabbits and otters who already knew Fish-Breath. A beaver in the far corner, who had once gotten quite belligerent when Fish-Breath refused to let her try wearing his presumably mechanical wings herself, guffawed loudly. Underneath the laughter, Witch-Hazel heard another, lower sound. Some kind of growling, followed by a hiss, but she couldn't place it.

The laughter died down, and Fish-Breath pulled his cloak back over his wings, looking abashed. The hedgehog smiled wanly—a weak, pitying expression under his pointed nose—and said, "You had me going there for quite a while. Well done." He had taken his cue from the rest of the bar, and didn't believe Fish-Breath anymore either. In fact, his nervous demeanor suggested he felt embarrassed by his earlier gullibility.

Witch-Hazel reached out and took hold of Fish-Breath's nearest paw. It happened to be the one with the Moon Opal embedded in his furry knuckle between the webbing connecting his fingers. His large paw felt warm in hers, except for the cool, smooth gemstone. "Come on," she said, giving his paw a tug. She wanted to defend him, the way she knew he would always defend her, but she'd seen this situation play out before. Nothing good would come from staying in the bar at this point. "Let's get out of here. Go find Twiggy, and bring her some dinner."

Fish-Breath nodded agreeably. Though his whole demeanor had changed, as if the barroom's laughter had been a bucket of cold water poured on a cheerfully burning fire. He was all soggy ashes now. Disappointment radiated from his slumped shoulders, downturned whiskers, and brooding frown.

He pulled his paw away, but as he did, Witch-Hazel felt a zinging zap, like a tiny bolt of static electricity, from the Moon Opal. She rubbed her paws together, trying to drive the sting away, but the feeling grew, warm and tingling in the nerves inside her claw tips. She thought she saw silver sparks crackling in the space cupped between her hands, and several petals pulled off the nearby hedgehog's back spines, floating through the air towards her. But then the sparkles and the tingling died away, and the petals dropped gracefully to the floor.

Witch-Hazel wasn't sure what she had seen. Or what she had done.

Unaware of the squirrel's minor mystery, Fish-Breath gathered up a satchel of food to bring to Twiggy. Witch-Hazel followed him out of the bar, back into the night, still staring at her paws, too distracted to notice either the low growling sound as they exited the tavern or the pair of glowing yellow eyes, staring greedily at them from the shadows.

2

As they walked through the town, Witch-Hazel told Fish-Breath about the strange sensation she'd felt after touching the Moon Opal embedded in his paw. "It's hard to describe," she said. "It felt … it felt like holding moon-dust in my paws."

"Was it magic, do you think?" Fish-Breath asked.

"Maybe."

Witch-Hazel had encountered magic before, but usually at a distance. She'd seen others use magic. She'd never felt it within the palms of her own paws before, almost as if it were a power she was conjuring and controlling herself. Still, she couldn't think of any other explanation.

Beyond the outskirts of Riverton, Fish-Breath and Twiggy kept a small camp—a few hammocks strung between trees, the remains of a cooking fire they rekindled most nights, and the giant basket of Twiggy's hot air balloon, turned on its side to provide a small shelter if it rained. Not that Fish-Breath or Twiggy minded the rain. Otters and beavers love to feel water running over their thick, dense fur. But Witch-Hazel appreciated the upended basket. She didn't like her fluffy, silvery tail to get soggy. Her fur was too soft and delicate to do anything but absorb the water, letting it soak right to the skin underneath.

They arrived at the camp to find Twiggy all in a tizzy. The industrious beaver had righted the basket for the hot air balloon, and she seemed to be gathering up all her tools and mechanical supplies that were usually strewn around the campsite in various stages of use and disuse. Witch-Hazel was afraid to ever touch them, for fear of destroying some delicate machine Twiggy was working on. But now, the beaver was moving back and forth between a chest carved into the base of a nearby tree trunk they used for locking up valuables, and the hot air balloon's basket, seemingly dithering over how to divide her tools between them.

"What's going on?" Fish-Breath asked.

"Packing," Twiggy answered abruptly. Her buck teeth whistled, as they often did when she felt stressed.

The beaver had already unstrung the hammocks. Witch-Hazel saw them folded neatly and stacked in the corner of the basket. Their homey campsite had transformed into hardly more than a burnt out fire surrounded by pawprints now. Twiggy was serious.

"What happened?" Witch-Hazel asked.

At the same time, Fish-Breath asked, "Why?"

Twiggy stopped her dithering and looked at them. She sighed deeply, whistling through her teeth again; set down the tools she'd been holding; and brushed her paws nervously on the frills of her yellow sundress. "I went to see my mentor."

"The tortoise?" Fish-Breath asked.

Twiggy nodded.

"Who's the tortoise?" Witch-Hazel asked.

"She's the oldest creature … well, anywhere, really." Fish-Breath's round face squinched in thought. "If you're not counting gods like the All-Being," he amended.

"So, like, half of the people we've dealt with on our travels," Witch-Hazel quipped, remembering half a dozen gods, ghosts, and mythical creatures who she'd personally faced.

Twiggy's teeth whistled impatiently, and the other two quieted, waiting for her to continue. In the momentary stillness, Witch-Hazel thought she heard the same growling again that had underlined the laughter at the tavern. She looked around, but still couldn't place it.

"Merry-Green says the greatest surgeon in the world is an octopus living among the volcanic vents off the coast of the Isle of Gryffindell. If anyone can safely remove the Celestial Fragments from Fish-Breath's body, it's this octopus. We must go to her."

"Why now?" Witch-Hazel objected. As she spoke, the indistinct growling rose in volume. Her silver tail whipped about like a flag in a strong wind, expressing her concern and raw nerves.

Witch-Hazel didn't want to leave Riverton. She didn't want to see Fish-Breath go under a surgeon's knife, no matter how skilled. And she didn't like that growling. Where *was* it coming from?

"Could the surgeon cut off my wings too?" Fish-Breath asked, spreading his tawny wings wide enough his cloak slipped down between them, gathering into a narrow cape along his spine.

Witch-Hazel's breath caught at the sight of his wings. He hid them so often, and yet they were so beautiful. The feathers ranged from long, golden-brown pinions all the way to soft, fluffy bits of cream-colored down. A few times since moving to Riverton, the three friends had toasted marshmallows over their campfire, and the color of Fish-Breath's wings made Witch-Hazel think of all the creamy golden shades of those sweet confections as they'd roasted over the flames, slowly browning to perfection.

Fish-Breath, with his magnificent wings, was perfection.

"Why would you cut off your wings?" Witch-Hazel sighed.

Fish-Breath frowned, still holding his wings wide. The petulant expression on his usually jolly face made him look even more charming, practically begging a squirrel to turn all goofy in hopes of cheering him up.

The Otter's Wings

"Otters don't have wings," he said simply, before snapping the wings—which belied the simplicity of his statement through their mere existence—shut across his back, tangling the cloak in their folds. He had to flap them several times to untangle the cloak enough to spread it across his back again, hiding the beautiful wings from sight.

As he pulled the cloak tight around himself, the Star Sliver embedded in Fish-Breath's wrist gleamed, twinkling with shining light, and just before he covered the topaz Sun Shard on his chest, its facets danced with the glow of sunlight, as if the gemstones responded to his feelings.

The growl Witch-Hazel couldn't place rose to a roar, and something leapt out from behind a thicket of blackberry brambles, causing a cold shadow to sweep past her. The shadow had weight and presence, knocking the squirrel off her paws on its way. The dark figure rushed straight to Fish-Breath, and tangled with the otter, clawing at his cloak, tearing long rents in the fabric. As soon as Fish-Breath struggled free, he unfolded his wings and escaped upward, flapping his way into the night sky, leaving his discarded cloak in the shadow's paws.

It all happened so quickly—Witch-Hazel hardly understood how she'd gone from talking to her friend to staring at a feline form prowling angrily through their campsite, growling and swishing its tail. The cat had felt solid enough when it knocked Witch-Hazel aside, but looking at it now, the creature was translucent, immaterial, seemingly made from the shadows themselves, except for its glowing yellow eyes.

The shadowcat stared upward, glaring at the otter flying just above the level of the treetops. Too high for the cat to reach. Although, for a moment, Witch-Hazel feared the cat's shadowy paws would lift off the ground, float up, and chase Fish-Breath away from them, far into the starry sky.

Because why shouldn't a cat built from shadows be able to float into the sky?

But instead, the shadowcat prowled in circles on the ground under Fish-Breath, growling and glaring.

With a quick exchange of glances and head tilts, Witch-Hazel and Twiggy agreed to back away, slowly, silently, from the fierce feline form. They stepped with quiet paws, not turning away from the cat, because neither of them wanted it behind them. They backed up to the tree with the chest carved in its trunk.

Moving as carefully as she could, Witch-Hazel grabbed her own satchel that Twiggy had leaned against the base of the tree. It was lightweight, mostly empty. She slung it over her shoulder and then whispered under her breath to Twiggy, "The shadow doesn't seem interested in us. Just him."

Fish-Breath was flapping his wings and hovering above their campsite, looking lost and bewildered.

"He doesn't know what to do," Twiggy whispered back. "We have to choose a plan."

Witch-Hazel's heart was already beating rapidly from her fear of the shadowcat. *What exactly was it? Where had it come from? And what did it want with Fish-Breath? Was it after the Celestial Fragments keeping him alive? It must be.* Nonetheless, Witch-Hazel's heart sped up as she realized this was the moment when she needed to give in to Twiggy's plans. The beaver had a plan. And Witch-Hazel didn't.

So Twiggy's plan would have to do. At least, for now. When there was time to argue, maybe they could change direction.

"Whatever that thing is," Witch-Hazel whispered, "it can't seem to fly. If we leave, like you wanted, heading toward that island, we can escape it. Then maybe there will be time to figure out what it is."

Twiggy nodded. "I can't …" She looked helplessly at her hot air balloon, deflated and lying on the ground on the far side of the terrifying, chilling shadow beast.

Witch-Hazel's heart raced even faster as she said, "I'll climb the tree. Fish-Breath will come to me. I know he will, and I'm small enough for him to carry." As a normally-sized squirrel, Witch-Hazel was barely half of Fish-Breath's river otter height. "I'll have him fly toward the ocean, far enough to be safe. That … thing … will follow us, giving you a chance to get the balloon ready. Then you come find us? You'll catch up to us. You have to, because he won't be able to keep flying forever."

Twiggy nodded again and whispered, "I'll be fast."

This time the beaver's teeth whistled on the final word, and the shadowcat's immaterial head snapped around to look at them, fixing them with a yellow-eyed stare that made Witch-Hazel's legs feel rubbery. She was reminded of the golden eyes of a snake she'd stared into long ago.

She wished she still had the sword that had been in her paws the last time she'd seen eyes like these. But she hadn't needed weapons in a long time, and there were none at hand.

Suddenly, the shadowcat leapt toward them, and without a single thought, Witch-Hazel turned tail and scurried up the tree. It was a ponderosa pine with a wide trunk that ran straight up for a long time before reaching any branches. Twiggy would have no chance of following her, but hopefully the shadowcat would be distracted from the stout, stolid beaver on the ground by the sight of a silvery squirrel tail waving like a flag, heading toward the winged otter in the sky.

Witch-Hazel ran straight up the tree, not stopping to look back, not even when the shadowcat's growls peaked into yowling howls. Nothing alive should be able to make sounds like that. But then, Witch-Hazel wasn't sure if the shadowcat was alive. It almost seemed more like a trick of

The Otter's Wings

light and fear, all wrapped up together. More magic. But evil magic this time.

Witch-Hazel reached the pinnacle of the tree and after a quick glance to see the shadowcat was following her, rather than chasing after Twiggy, she called out to Fish-Breath. He swooped to her immediately, relief filling his face at the sight of her. His short arms wrapped around her middle, as he flew past, yanking her out of the tree and into the empty space between tree, ground, and sky. The tight grasp knocked the air out of her lungs, and it took the squirrel a moment to find her voice again.

Witch-Hazel cried out, "Fly toward the ocean!" As she spoke, she grabbed her own paws tightly onto Fish-Breath's webbed ones, reinforcing his hold on her.

Her paw pads brushed against both the Star Sliver in his wrist and the Moon Opal on his knuckle. She could also feel the Sun Shard embedded in his chest against her back. All three gems tingled against her, electrifying, like they were charging her up with a magic of her own.

Or maybe ... that was just the dizzying thrill of flying.

Witch-Hazel was flying.

3

EACH FLAP OF FISH-BREATH'S WINGS pulled them higher into the sky and farther away from Riverton. The wings weren't hers, but Witch-Hazel could feel their movements. It made her feel like she was the one who was flying.

Though as the world disappeared into darkness beneath them, realization crept into Witch-Hazel's heart, starting as a shivery feeling under her fur: if Fish-Breath were to let go of her—lose his grip, or just decided he didn't care about carrying her anymore—she'd fall farther than she could survive falling. She grabbed onto him harder, and the facets of the Star Sliver embedded in his wrist cut sharply against her paw. As it did, she felt lighter, almost as if she were floating and didn't need Fish-Breath to carry her.

The Star Sliver was the gem that granted Fish-Breath the power of flight. It was the gem that gave him his wings.

Witch-Hazel closed her eyes. She was getting giddy from the thin air if she thought merely touching the gemstone could give her a piece of its magic. The magic of the gems was embedded in Fish-Breath's body. Magic wasn't that fickle.

Or was it?

Witch-Hazel squeezed her eyes tightly closed. It did no good to look at the terrifying distance beneath her when she had no power to do anything about it. She asked, "Are we heading toward the ocean?"

Her voice felt like it was whipped away by the wind as soon as she used it. But Fish-Breath must have heard, because he leaned his mouth down, close to her pointed ears and said, "I'm following the river. It'll take us there."

Witch-Hazel nodded mutely, even though he couldn't possibly see the gesture. Then she said, "Twiggy will follow with the balloon."

Fish-Breath didn't respond, but Witch-Hazel trusted he'd heard her. After a while, she relaxed in his paws. She even risked opening her eyes and saw he'd flown much lower, much closer to the treetops. The river glinted in the moonlight like a dark snake with shining black scales. She stared intently at the treetops passing beneath them, trying to learn what different types of trees looked like from above, muted to shades of gray by the night. Eventually, she realized, they were flying over an oak grove, and she could have sworn she saw the very tree she'd grown up in.

Witch-Hazel almost asked Fish-Breath to stop. But she didn't know how fast the shadowcat could travel. It was safer to stay in the air until Twiggy joined them. And yet ...

Regardless of safety, Fish-Breath's wings and arms were tiring. She could tell from the way he kept shifting his grip around her waist and how they lurched unevenly through the air.

"Fish-Breath," she said, "I know the oak grove we just passed. My family lives there." She was giving him an out. An excuse to take a break and stop flying.

He couldn't fly forever. And for whatever reason, Twiggy hadn't joined them in the air yet. She'd had more than enough time to fill the hot air balloon by now, but perhaps the winds had been fickle and given her trouble.

Witch-Hazel hoped their beaver friend was okay. She hated to think of the shadowcat turning on her—Twiggy wasn't a fighter.

But she also wasn't encrusted with magical gemstones.

Whatever the shadowcat wanted, wherever it had come from, it had seemed to be after Fish-Breath specifically, and that meant it was probably after the gemstones, which if returned to the All-Being in her castle, could stop magic draining from the world.

Maybe the shadowcat was made from magic, and it needed the cracks in the celestial bodies to stop draining magic, or it would die.

If so, Witch-Hazel hoped it would die soon. She still had mixed feelings about the idea of magic draining from the world. Magic hadn't always been a boon in her own life.

Fish-Breath swooped back to the oak grove and landed on a thick branch near the top of a tree Witch-Hazel recognized. The last time she'd been home, one of her sisters had a nest in this tree.

Once Witch-Hazel's claws had firmly dug into the bark of the oak branch, Fish-Breath let go of her. He immediately wobbled, leaning dangerously one way and another as he tried to get his balance. Otters aren't meant for treetops, even if they have wings. Witch-Hazel turned and grabbed ahold of one of his arms, steadying him.

"Thank you," Fish-Breath said. "I … didn't know if the ground was safe."

"Cats can usually climb trees," Witch-Hazel pointed out. "One made from shadows … well, it should have even less trouble."

An almost comical expression of fear painted itself across Fish-Breath's face, and Witch-Hazel was filled with the need to comfort him.

"But I'm sure it couldn't have travelled this far, this fast …" The squirrel trailed off, realizing she might be lying. She wasn't sure of anything when it came to translucent beings made from shadows rolled up into the shape of a cat. "I wish we knew more about that thing."

Fish-Breath's wings drooped wearily at his sides. He was a funny looking fellow at the best of times, with his long body, shorter limbs, and round face with small eyes and a big round nose. Just like any river otter. But right now? Perched awkwardly at the top of a tree? Witch-Hazel had trouble not laughing at him, even though she would never want to hurt his feelings.

Still … He would understand how funny he looked. She let herself chuckle a little, and in response, his distressed expression quirked, cracking a lopsided smile.

"Is that the first time you've flown since being in the All-Being's realm?" Witch-Hazel asked.

Fish-Breath dawdled about answering and was saved from having to by the appearance of another squirrel on a lower branch peering up at them. "Hello," he called down. "Do you have a nest or something where we could rest? I may have wings, but I'm not very comfortable up here, and I'm afraid to go down to the ground."

The other squirrel stared at Fish-Breath in stunned astonishment until Witch-Hazel interceded. "Daffodil? Is that you? You still live here?"

"Witch-Hazel!?" the other squirrel exclaimed. "We all thought we'd never see you again!"

"Yes, Daffy, it's me." Witch-Hazel felt a flash of shame over how she'd left her family—nothing but a cryptic note, claiming she'd gone adventuring, for her siblings to find. But then she felt a flash of pride over how she'd returned—in the company of a wonderful, magically enhanced otter, after having adventured deep under the ground and high into the sky. She'd met the All-Being. She'd fought battles. She'd rescued friends and slain enemies. She had nothing to be ashamed of. And yet, if the lesson of Riverton had taught her anything, her sisters and brothers here wouldn't believe the stories she had to tell.

Well ... Maybe. They hadn't known Fish-Breath and his jokes or Twiggy and her inventions beforehand. None of them would think Witch-Hazel was capable of weaving such an elaborate prank as to render a normal river otter into the appearance of a mythical creature.

"My nest is a few branches down," Daffodil said, uncertainly. "Do ... do you need help getting your friend down there?"

"I think I can manage," Fish-Breath said.

But then he wobbled on the branch again, and Witch-Hazel said, "Yes, please."

Daffodil scurried up to them and took hold of Fish-Breath's other arm, all while looking dazzled by the sight of his wings. They were dazzling. Between the two of them, the squirrels managed to help the tired, clumsy otter climb down the curving branches to where Daffodil's nest was built against the trunk of the tree.

Unlike Witch-Hazel, Daffodil had always been good at weaving bits of grass, twigs, and papery dry leaves into a cozy nest. The woven plant matter curved all the way around, creating a comfortable hollow space, tight against the chilly nighttime air. The space was large enough for an entire litter of squirrel kits, though there were no young ones at present. Witch-Hazel realized the nieces and nephews she remembered must have already grown up and gone off to make nests of their own. She felt a pang of longing over having missed the ends of their childhoods.

Daffodil's home was a large space for a squirrel nest, but Fish-Breath still had to hunker down, slumping his shoulders, and curling his wings in tightly against his back. Even so, he barely fit inside, but Daffodil had always been a gracious, kind host, and she didn't complain. Back in the day when Witch-Hazel had lived in this grove, struggling to make nests of her own—always tattered affairs that fell apart at the behest of the lightest breeze—she had regularly mooched off of her sisters and brothers, crashing at their more soundly constructed nests. And because of her kindness, Daffodil had always borne the brunt of Witch-Hazel's dependence.

"Should I go dig up a stash of nuts?" Daffodil asked, eying the otter. She was probably wondering how much a large creature like him would eat and hoping he wasn't hungry.

Fish-Breath had, in fact, already closed his eyes and started snoring softly through his whiskers. Flying must have exhausted him more than Witch-Hazel would have guessed. She supposed much of that was her fault ... His wings weren't meant to carry both him and an additional squirrel, even if she was less than half his size.

"I think we're okay," Witch-Hazel answered, demurring the offer of sustenance.

Daffodil chittered. "Liar," she said. "I've never known my wander-lost sister to not be hungry. And that otter looks half starved by whatever you've done to him."

"What I've done to him?!" Witch-Hazel exclaimed in outrage. Daffodil knew nothing of her sister's life over the last year, but she already felt safe making assumptions. Years of memories rolled over Witch-Hazel, years of being the troublesome, burdensome sister. The one they called 'wander-lost,' long before she'd actually lost herself to wandering and had only been accusing her of indulging in too many daydreams.

"I'll be right back." Daffodil scurried out.

Witch-Hazel leaned out of the nest and watched her favorite sister descend down the trunk of the oak tree. She sighed. Daffodil really would be back soon. She probably knew exactly where every stash of nuts she'd ever hidden could be found, and she could go straight to them. Witch-Hazel had never understood that sorcery. Once she buried a stash of nuts, it might as well have crumbled into dirt for all the luck she'd ever had digging them back up.

Being back home was strange. She felt young and incompetent again, in a way she hadn't felt in a long time. With Fish-Breath and Twiggy, she'd come to think of herself as a great defender, a warrior even. She wasn't mechanically smart like Twiggy, and she didn't know how to cook or make everyone laugh like Fish-Breath. But she knew how to take care of her friends and keep them safe, even when zombies or crazed eagles attacked them, or unicorns cast befuddling spells over them, tampering with their very senses.

Daffodil returned as quickly as Witch-Hazel expected, carrying a sack of mixed nuts over her shoulder. Witch-Hazel could make out the meaty smell of acorns, the woody smell of hazelnuts, and the slightly bitter scent of walnuts. All in the same bag. She'd forgotten how Daffodil liked to carefully organize the nuts she gathered into nicely mixed stashes, so she could have an array of flavors available, even if she only dug up one hidden stash.

Witch-Hazel loved that detail-oriented thinking in Daffodil. It also made her feel completely inadequate, like a defective creature who'd never quite been meant to be a squirrel.

For the next few hours, Witch-Hazel talked to Daffodil, catching up on all the details of the lives she'd been missing: sisters, brothers, nieces, nephews, and niblings all living their lives in the oak grove. The stories Daffodil told filled Witch-Hazel with a complicated mix of regret and relief. She felt sorrow, missing out on her family's growth and endeavors, but she would have found staying here—gathering nuts and building nests, playing with her siblings' kits and helping raise them—extremely stifling. She wouldn't trade her own life, complete with its dangers, for the domestic life of a simple squirrel, staying inside the sphere they'd been born into.

A few times, Witch-Hazel tried to tell Daffodil about her own life and adventures, but her sister replied, "Oh, your life sounds very exciting!" in a way that managed to sound both impressed and dismissive at the same time. A reply that confused Witch-Hazel.

Unlike the residents of Riverton, Daffodil didn't disbelieve Witch-Hazel's stories. She simply didn't seem to want to hear them. Perhaps they were too frightening? Or maybe, for once, Daffodil felt intimidated by Witch-Hazel, instead of the other way around, and she didn't know how to handle the feeling. Maybe the idea of a world as large and complicated as the one Witch-Hazel's stories implied threatened Daffodil's worldview. There was more to the world than a single oak grove.

It made Witch-Hazel sad that Daffodil didn't want to hear about her life, but she couldn't force her sister to be interested in her. So, Witch-Hazel held her tongue and listened instead. She likely wouldn't get another chance to hear about the domestic adventures of her family in their oak grove again.

Fish-Breath stayed asleep, and after a while, the two squirrels napped too, leaned against the otter's broad chest.

There was something deeply serene and restful, yet eerily surreal, about sleeping in Daffodil's nest, tangled up in the warm arms and tail of her sister again. Squeezed back into a world grown too small for her.

Witch-Hazel could have been content in that moment forever, half asleep and half awake, half in childhood and half an adult in the midst of her own adventures.

Then she heard the growling again.

4

WITCH-HAZEL FELT Fish-Breath's stillness subtly shift from the peaceful repose of sleep to the tense posture of someone waiting and listening. He could hear the growling too.

"We have to go." Fish-Breath's voice was low, ragged, and urgent.

Witch-Hazel tried to soothe him, saying, "It might not be the shadowcat ..." But as she peered out through the entrance to Daffodil's nest, she saw movement below.

Tangled up in the thick shadows of the tree's branches in the growing twilight of morning, there was another shadow. It wasn't natural; not cast by anything physical. And it moved, as if jumping from one branch's shadow to the next, climbing up the tree's shadow like a squirrel would climb the tree itself.

It was the shadowcat. Already here. And though the tree was tall, and its shadow even taller in the long light of pre-dawn, the unnatural shadow was climbing fast.

"You're right," Witch-Hazel admitted. She shrugged her satchel, freshly filled with the nuts Daffodil had brought up to the nest, over her shoulder.

Daffodil blinked at her guests, barely awake, and confused by them rousing so early.

"I'm sorry, sister," Witch-Hazel said. "But we have to leave."

"Now?" Daffodil asked, bleary.

"Now." Fish-Breath breathed the word like an incantation, a hope put into voice that they'd make it away in time. And he gripped Witch-Hazel around the middle, wings already rising from his back like extra-angular shoulder blades.

"Wait," Witch-Hazel said, squirming out of his arms and twisting toward him. "Let me climb on your back this time. It'll be easier for you, if we have to fly for long."

She knew they were both hoping Twiggy would find them soon. Once Fish-Breath took to the air, surely the bright rainbow colors of the beaver's hot air balloon would shine in the distance, too garish to hide behind any cloud. And yet ... it was better to be prepared for a long flight.

Fish-Breath nodded in agreement and climbed out of the squirrel nest.

"Goodbye, Daffodil," Witch-Hazel said. "And thank you." Then she followed her beloved, stoic otter into the chilly outside air, and as soon as he felt her small paws wrap firmly around his thick neck, Fish-Breath flapped his wings and rose into the air like a hawk.

Except, Fish-Breath wasn't a bird of prey; he wasn't the one doing the hunting. He was being hunted. And he

The Otter's Wings

shrieked in pain as the shadowcat slashed his rudder-like tail, arriving close enough to claw him with a shadowy paw only a moment before his wings carried him out of reach.

Witch-Hazel craned her neck around to see what damage the shadowcat had wrought, but she couldn't see his tail closely. Not without dangerously loosening her grip. So, all she could tell was that he was bleeding. The fur of his tail looked damp with blood, and droplets fell like tiny rubies from the tip of his tail, falling to the ground. Leaving a trail behind them.

"Get to the river," Witch-Hazel whispered into his round ear, and he banked in the air, shifting direction. Once Fish-Breath was flying over the river, the rushing water below would wash the trail away.

But that didn't stop him from bleeding.

Of course, the river was its own trail of sorts, and as the sun rose, Witch-Hazel watched the ground below them, trying to see shadows that didn't belong. She was half-convinced she could see the shadowcat, leaping from treetop to treetop along the riverside, following them in a way only a supernatural being could. Worse, sometimes, Witch-Hazel thought she saw more than one. At the height of her fear, she was sure there were five, leaping unnaturally long distances and keeping pace by jumping from shadow to shadow along the Earth below.

Riding on Fish-Breath's warm, solid back with the wind rustling along her own back and tail would have been comfortable—pleasant, even—if she weren't constantly worried about the shadowcats below and the otter's flagging strength. The swinging rhythm of his flight was soothing. But he was exhausted. And he was losing blood. And she didn't know how much. And there was nothing she could do to help, except whisper the occasional words of reassurance and encouragement in his ear.

But the farther they flew, the hollower those words sounded to her. Eventually, she couldn't bring herself to say them anymore.

Witch-Hazel felt like she was holding her breath, waiting for the rainbow colors of Twiggy's balloon to appear anywhere on the horizon, desperately waiting to exclaim at the happy sight. She kept peering at clouds, trying to imagine dim colors hidden inside or behind their cottony whiteness. Sometimes, she stared at especially tall trees, wondering and pushing herself to believe their branches might be obscuring her view of a giant rainbow balloon.

But of course, the balloon wasn't there. It wasn't hard to see.

When the hot air balloon finally appeared on the horizon, there was no question—no peering and imagining and hoping. It was just there, and Witch-Hazel's relief was palpable. She could feel Fish-Breath's relief too in the rhythm of his wings. Their regular beats smoothed from

The Otter's Wings

the frantic rhythm of a racing heartbeat to the gentle sighing of calm breaths.

"We've almost made it," Witch-Hazel whispered in his ear. "Only a little longer now." She kept whispering all the words of encouragement that had built up inside of her, as the hot air balloon grew larger and closer, until finally Fish-Breath crashed into the hanging basket, rolling in a tumble onto its floor.

"What kept you?" Fish-Breath gasped at the beaver standing over them. His wings sprawled and flopped across his heaving body. He was too tired to fold them up.

Witch-Hazel crawled out from under the melted otter and said to Twiggy, "Did the shadowcats give you trouble?"

"No," Twiggy said, kneeling down to examine Fish-Breath's bleeding tail. "Not like they seem to have given you. But the wind is fitful, and while my balloon is outfitted with rudder-sails to let me steer, I still depend on catching the wind for momentum."

Witch-Hazel dug through the various bags and baskets of supplies until she found some makeshift material for bandaging Fish-Breath's tail and some salted fish for him to eat. He'd need food to regain his strength after the marathon he'd spent all day and much of last night flying. And while the nuts Daffodil had given her were something, she knew Fish-Breath would be happier eating fish.

Twiggy went back to steering the balloon, and Witch-Hazel tended to Fish-Breath's tail—first washing it with a little peach cider from a flask and then wrapping it tightly in a piece of gauze. "It's still bleeding," she said. "Much more than it should be."

"What do you mean?" Twiggy asked.

"The shadowcat clawed me hours ago," Fish-Breath said. "The wound shouldn't be bleeding like it's still fresh."

"I think it's more than a normal cut," Witch-Hazel said. "The shadowcats are clearly supernatural. The touch of their claws must be too."

"Great," Twiggy snapped sarcastically. "Now the octopus surgeon needs to heal a supernatural wound as well as removing the Celestial Fragments."

"And my wings," Fish-Breath said.

"The shadowcat would've caught you without your wings," Witch-Hazel pointed out.

"The shadowcat wouldn't want me in the first place without them and these blasted gems." Fish-Breath rubbed his paws together, worrying the claws of one paw against the Moon Opal embedded in one of the knuckles of the other.

Witch-Hazel wrapped her small paws around the otter's bigger, webbed ones, stilling them. "Don't claw yourself," she said. "You don't need to lose more blood."

"I want to rip them out," Fish-Breath said. "If I had a knife, I'd try to cut the gems out myself."

"And what if you died without them?" Witch-Hazel stared steadily at Fish-Breath, until his angry gaze faltered, and he looked away.

Fish-Breath had never seemed angry or moody or brooding before they'd returned to Riverton. Witch-Hazel almost wondered if the Celestial Fragments had poisoned him somehow, filling his body with a magic it wasn't meant to hold, and changing him at a deeper level than could be seen with the eye.

Witch-Hazel touched the Moon Opal on his knuckle, gingerly and carefully. She felt the prickle of magic again.

The Moon Opal gave Fish-Breath endless breath. Perhaps he could live without the flight bestowed on him by the Star Sliver in his wrist. But …

Witch-Hazel didn't know if his body could live without the strength granted to him by the Sun Shard in his chest or the endless breath from the Moon Opal. She could still remember him gasping for breath, bleeding from his neck, dying in her arms after a zombie badger had sunk its teeth in his throat.

"I hope the octopus surgeon can help with the slice on your tail, but I wouldn't get your hopes up about the gems." Witch-Hazel said the words softly, and the rising wind pushing the hot air balloon toward the ocean tore them away before Fish-Breath had to hear them.

But Twiggy heard. And the beaver frowned.

Witch-Hazel didn't know if Twiggy was upset by the idea of the octopus surgeon failing, or if she was simply angry Witch-Hazel doubted her plan. But the beaver had gotten her way. They were flying toward the mysterious octopus surgeon, whether Witch-Hazel liked it or not. So, there was no point in arguing any more.

All they could do was fly toward the ocean and hope they'd find help there.

5

As the day waned, Witch-Hazel alternated between peering over the edge of the hot air balloon's basket to watch for tell-tale shadows far below them on the ground; fussing over Fish-Breath's tail as it soaked one bandage after another through with blood; and trying to cheer up the wilting otter with snacks and stories.

Twiggy stayed resolutely focused on steering the balloon. Witch-Hazel suspected the balloon didn't require that degree of focus, based on her previous experiences with flying in it. However, she could sympathize with the beaver's need to focus on something less scary than Fish-Breath's wound and the shadows chasing them. The squirrel wouldn't have minded a distraction of her own, but she had to make do with steeling herself by focusing on how much Fish-Breath needed her to stay strong for him.

As the sun descended through the final quarter of the sky, dimming the world and reddening the clouds on the horizon, Witch-Hazel tasted salt in her whiskers. It permeated the air. The ocean was getting closer. She'd heard of it—mostly in Fish-Breath's tall tales and stories—but in all her travels, she'd never been there.

The idea of the ocean—an expanse of water so wide it cut the world in half, stretching across the entire horizon like a sunrise or sunset—seemed almost as far-fetched and magical to her as a beanstalk that rose all the way up to a castle in the clouds. At least, she had seen the beanstalk and the castle in the clouds. She had laid her paws on them, felt her claws sink into the beanstalk's fleshy vines and scrape the marble floors of the castle.

Perhaps others laughed at those legends. But they were real to her.

The ocean? It wasn't real until she looked over the edge of the hot air balloon's basket and found herself puzzled by the thickness of the clouds in the distance and the way they blocked out the view of the ground. Then she realized she wasn't looking at thick, slate gray clouds cutting across the horizon, growing darker with every minute now that the sun had set.

It was the sea.

The water of the ocean was flatter than she'd expected. Surely, there were crashing waves somewhere; perhaps they'd becomes visible when the hot air balloon got closer. For now, though, there was simply a great, smooth expanse of grayness bleeding into the edge of the gray, cloudy sky., and they were heading right toward it.

The Otter's Wings

The surface of the water dimpled in places, by wind or currents underneath; Witch-Hazel wasn't sure exactly what she was seeing, but it was mesmerizing. She had never seen the horizon become such a clear, straight line before. It made the world seem larger. She wondered how it would feel when the hot air balloon floated directly above it.

The small squirrel, feeling smaller than ever before, stared at the sea for long moments, dumbstruck, before she found her tongue and managed to ask, "Is that it? Is that the ocean?"

Fish-Breath moved, twisting and craning. "Help me up," he said, eagerness and life returning to him. "I want to see."

"You shouldn't move too much," Witch-Hazel fussed, her attention drawn back to the tragedy unfolding within the tiny sphere of the basket. "It might make the bleeding worse."

"No," Twiggy said firmly. Witch-Hazel thought the beaver was agreeing with her. Then she added, "He needs to see."

Twiggy tied the ropes she'd been using to steer in place and knelt down to help Fish-Breath climb up enough to lean on the basket's edge, front paws draped over the side.

The widest grin filled Fish-Breath's face. He hadn't looked happier since before Riverton. "The sea," he sighed, and the word carried so much joy and contentment that

Witch-Hazel wished she could live inside the single syllable. She could live a lifetime there.

"You've never seen it before either," Witch-Hazel said. She hadn't realized.

Beneath most of Fish-Breath's tall tales lay kernels of truth, and somehow, Witch-Hazel had assumed the otter and beaver had traveled to the ocean before. They had always been more worldly than her, better educated, and more widely traveled.

But here, they were all new.

"The wind is rising," Fish-Breath said, still staring at the sea like it was his true home, even though he'd never seen it before. "We're almost there."

Witch-Hazel felt the salty air sting her eyes as it whipped through the space between the basket and the balloon above. She looked up into the yawning, rainbowed space inside the balloon above them and saw the wind contorting its shape, pressing it out of true, changing the cheerful roundness into a harried asymmetry.

Witch-Hazel looked down from staring at the balloon's colorful interior to see Twiggy wrestling with the ropes controlling it. Then she looked out at the dimming scene beneath them and based on the way trees and rocky outcroppings rushed by, she realized they could be in real trouble.

"The wind is pushing us down the beach," Witch-Hazel said. "Is that a problem?"

The Otter's Wings

"Do you need help?" Fish-Breath asked even though he was in no condition to provide help. And Witch-Hazel was so much smaller than either the otter or the struggling beaver; she wouldn't be much use at wrestling with the ropes for steering the balloon.

"It'll be fine," Twiggy said through gritted teeth, an impressive feat with teeth like hers. "Once we get past the coastal breeze and over the open ocean, the winds will die down."

Witch-Hazel wasn't sure if Twiggy was speaking from knowledge, perhaps information passed on to her from Merry-Green the tortoise mentor, or if her certainty was bred purely from the combination of hope and wishful thinking. Either way, it didn't seem helpful to question her.

So, Witch-Hazel huddled on the floor of the basket, beside Fish-Breath, both of them hiding from the wind. She held his webbed paw, squeezing it and rubbing her paw pads over the Moon Opal in his knuckle, feeling the electric spark of the gemstone against her skin. The feeling grew stronger each time her thumb passed over the smooth stone, tickling at first, but then burning in her paws, like she could shoot fire from her claw tips if she needed to. If it would help her protect Fish-Breath, or steer the balloon to safety, or vanquish those terrifying shadow-cats.

The basket rocked, and Twiggy swore, something Witch-Hazel had never heard her do before. But the rocking and swearing continued as the dim sky darkened to blackness and the stars emerged.

Eventually, the swearing, rocking, and whipping wind died down. Witch-Hazel wasn't sure whether Twiggy had been right, and the wind was calmer over the open ocean, or if the wind had simply died with the dying of the day. Either way, the balloon floated peacefully over an eerily dark sea, stretching as far as Witch-Hazel could see in every direction, except for behind them, where the coastline dwindled away, barely visible in the darkness and growing ever smaller.

It would be horrible to be lost at sea. Nowhere to land. Trapped by a dizzying freedom to fly in any direction, but with nowhere worth going. Water all around, but all of it too salty to drink.

Worst of all, now that the world was wrapped in the darkness of night, everything had turned to shadows, and Witch-Hazel feared the shadowcats could be anywhere and leap out to attack Fish-Breath and finish him off at any moment. She'd seen them travel from one shadow to the next, jumping between them as if shadows were their true realm of existence, and not the physical world.

Yet, she hoped, desperately and fervently, that the shadowcats had been left behind when the balloon drifted past the shoreline and out to sea. Cats don't like water.

The Otter's Wings

And before night fell, the ocean was a broad, flat expanse, with no trees to cast shadows upon it. The only shadows came from clouds or sea birds overhead, small drifting shadows. The shadowcats couldn't live in those, could they?

"You're so alert," Fish-Breath said softly.

"I can't rest," Witch-Hazel said. "I feel like the shadowcats could jump out at us from anywhere in this darkness."

Fish-Breath smiled, his body relaxing. "My protector. Who'd have thought a fierce little squirrel like you would become the bodyguard for a big oafish otter like me? I always feel safe when you're around. What did I do to deserve that?"

"Are you kidding?" Witch-Hazel asked. She knew he often was. He could even make a joke out of lying in the bottom of a basket, bleeding out. But she didn't feel like joking. "You're the mirror I want to see myself reflected in. Better than any reflection in water, no matter how still and deep. Better than the glass contraptions Twiggy makes—"

"Hey now," Twiggy objected perfunctorily.

"—Much better than my image of myself in my mind's eye. Though, I find that one improves when I'm around you …" *Even better than the All-Being reflecting her form, brightened from silver to gold.* Witch-Hazel thought the last part, but she didn't say it. "You have to survive this, because I need you, for me to be me."

"Look at you," Fish-Breath wheezed, clearly in pain and trying to ignore it. "Knowing exactly what to say to cheer a glum otter like me up, making me feel all important and everything just for looking at you. What would I do without you?" His words slowed with drowsiness.

Witch-Hazel laughed. Here, she'd thought she was being selfish, making Fish-Breath's ordeal all about herself, and the wonderful otter found a way to turn her image around on her yet again.

Witch-Hazel held Fish-Breath's paw tighter and focused on listening to his breathing. After only moments, he'd fallen asleep. And she tried to match her breathing to his, trying to quell the panic rising inside her.

Twiggy tied the steering ropes in place again, and settled on the floor of the basket beside the sleeping otter and quietly panicking squirrel.

"How do we find the octopus surgeon?" Witch-Hazel asked, her voice a hoarse whisper. She hoped her voice sounded sore from the windy sea air to Twiggy and not husky from fear. It would help no one to let on how frightened this journey made her. She needed to be strong for her friends.

"The octopus's lair is among the volcanic vents under the ocean beside the Isle of Gryffindell, remember? I told you before." Twiggy sounded very tired and very irritable. Those two feelings were probably strongly tied together.

The Otter's Wings

"Sorry," Witch-Hazel muttered, trying not to worry about the word "lair." It was not a promising word. It conjured images of evil mad scientists, doing horrifying experiments on their prey—not a helpful doctor who could cure her friend. But it was one word. And Merry-Green had sent them to find this octopus. Not that Witch-Hazel knew Merry-Green from a tortoise shaped rock …

After a while, unable to sleep and hearing from Twiggy's breathing that the beaver was still awake as well, Witch-Hazel risked asking, "How do we find the Isle of Gryffindell?"

"Merry-Green said it was one day's flight, straight into the ocean." Twiggy sounded uncertain, and Witch-Hazel could tell she didn't need to raise all the questions screaming at them from inside those vague directions: *how fast of a flight? How much of a day? What if the wind blew them off course? And how would they recognize the island? Would it be the only one? Was it too large to miss? What if they flew right past it, heading further and further out to sea, with no landmarks to guide them except the stars?*

"Can you read the stars?" Witch-Hazel asked. She knew from Fish-Breath's stories that sailors used the stars to guide them, a kind of map in the sky.

"A little," Twiggy answered.

"Show me?" Witch-Hazel asked.

So the squirrel and beaver soothed themselves by teaching and learning about the constellations in the night sky. Eventually, Twiggy taught Witch-Hazel how to work the steering ropes, as long as the wind stayed peaceful enough that the small squirrel wouldn't need a larger mammal's strength to wrestle with them. Then the two took turns sleeping and steering through the rest of the night, until dawn painted the sky yellow and the ocean gold.

Fish-Breath awoke with a wide yawn during one of Witch-Hazel's shifts to steer the balloon. She smiled at him, happy to see him waking up, but then the happiness balanced out with a pang of concern. She could see the bandage on his tail had soaked through with redness again.

"What's that?" Fish-Breath asked, pointing out at the sky, alarm and uncertainty painted across his face.

6

Witch-Hazel turned and saw a dark shape, silhouetted against the buttery dawn sky. It looked like a shadow, and with a shiver down her spine, Witch-Hazel realized it looked feline. It moved like a cat, graceful and flowing, but it flew like a bird among the pink and orange clouds.

The shadowcats had grown wings. And they were coming for Fish-Breath.

Next to Fish-Breath, Twiggy stirred and woke up too. She turned and looked at the sky, where Fish-Breath had been pointing, and then, sleepily, the beaver drawled, "Gryphon … it's a gryphon. We're almost there."

Startled by Twiggy's declaration, Witch-Hazel peered harder at the dark shape flying loops and cartwheels in the sky. It certainly moved in a much more cheerful and lively way than how the shadowcats had crept along the ground, leaping from shadow to shadow as if the rules of physics didn't apply to them. This shape had weight and substance.

Twiggy was right. The flying shape wasn't a mere shadow, it was a solid, corporeal creature, with the body and tail of a cat, but the wings and head of a falcon.

"Wait ... the Isle of Gryffindell *has actual gryphons?*" Witch-Hazel shouldn't have been surprised, after all the other mythical creatures she'd met, and yet, she was. She could still be surprised. Perhaps that was a good thing; she hadn't grown numb to the world. "I thought it was just a name," she muttered.

"No," Twiggy said. "There's an actual colony of gryphons there, according to Merry-Green."

"How does Merry-Green know?" Witch-Hazel asked. "Has she traveled there? Has she met the octopus surgeon?"

Twiggy got up from where she'd been sleeping on the floor of the basket, straightened and dusted off her sundress, and took the steering ropes from Witch-Hazel's paws. "No," she answered, finally. "Merry-Green never leaves her cave beside the lake south of Riverton, but she has connections with travelers and traders, and she tells me she's exchanged letters with the octopus surgeon. They've been pen pals for many years. The gryphons on Gryffindell Isle are part of the trade route that makes passing their letters back and forth possible."

Witch-Hazel tried to imagine an ancient tortoise living in a cave, sending letters by way of gryphon to an octopus surgeon, and somehow it seemed stranger to her than a unicorn living in a grove of lies or a snake raising zombies from the dead. It had such a pastoral quality—a quietness entirely mismatched to Witch-Hazel's experience of life ever since she'd first gone adventuring.

The Otter's Wings

The sky brightened and the gryphon grew easier to see. Then more gryphons became visible, coasting between the pink clouds in the powder blue sky. Their feline bodies were all different colors—some tabby, some splotched; in every shade of orange, white, and gray. Their heads and wings were more uniformly colored, mostly dark shades of brown or steel gray. Some of them had feline forelegs, but others had bird talons instead of front paws, more like a classical gryphon.

Witch-Hazel hadn't expected the gryphons' feline parts to look descended from house cats. She'd have expected lions, leopards, or something else equally wild. Also bigger. Although, from her perspective as a small squirrel, tabby cats were plenty big enough. Both the feline and avian halves of these mythical creatures made Witch-Hazel nervous. Without weapons, she'd be unlikely to win a fight with a house cat, and a falcon could swoop down from the sky and scoop her up like a tasty morsel.

Witch-Hazel didn't mind the world being so big, but she wasn't sure why so many of the creatures in it needed to be big too.

Big and fierce. With sharp claws and hooked beaks. The closer the hot air balloon drifted to the flock of gryphons, the more nervous they made Witch-Hazel.

"Did Merry-Green tell you the gryphons were …" Witch-Hazel was torn between asking if they were "safe" and "friendly." But she didn't get a chance to finish the sentence, so she didn't have to choose.

"No," Twiggy said. "All Merry-Green told me was they work for Occultus, the octopus surgeon." The beaver looked like she was beginning to think she should have asked her mentor more questions before leaving on this escapade.

The gryphons had begun circling the hot air balloon at a wary distance. All three of the travelers in the balloon's basket were keenly aware this meant there was no way out. The gryphons could block the balloon's passage through the sky from any direction.

The gryphons cawed and meowed, seemingly speaking to each other in a language the woodland animals didn't recognize. Perhaps it was an oceanic dialect? Or perhaps, they weren't talking at all; they were merely making noise and shrieking at something unusual in their usually placid, pacific corner of the world.

There was something strange and wrong about the gryphons. The way their wings connected to their backs didn't look natural; the angles were wrong, and they weren't consistent from one gryphon to the next. The wings looked less like limbs that had grown with their bodies and more like appendages that had been jammed on later.

The Otter's Wings

Worse, some of the gryphons' heads seemed to be twisted wrong, like they weren't on entirely straight, and so the gryphon could only look toward one side.

Witch-Hazel shuddered. "They make me think of the zombies the snake raised," she said, quietly to Fish-Breath. "You know, down in the church crypt, right before you ... died."

Fish-Breath squeezed her paw.

"I don't know why," Witch-Hazel said. Maybe Fish-Breath's unhealing wound had cast her mind back to that time and place, and as long as she feared for his life, she couldn't shake the feeling of being there. Maybe there was nothing wrong with the gryphons at all. Heaven knew she'd met strange creatures—like the half human, half lion leontaur—before. There was no reason for these gryphons to shake her up so badly.

"It's the smell," Twiggy said. "They smell wrong. Not quite dead. But ... deathly."

Witch-Hazel sniffed the fresh air gusting across the basket and realized Twiggy was right. Under the bright scent of salt from the sea and musty smell of the gryphons' feathers, there was a septic undertone.

One of the gryphons circled closer, and Witch-Hazel's body tensed in preparation for a fight. Though, fighting a gryphon midair, with only the open ocean beneath them, was a recipe for disaster. Even if they could win a fight on solid ground—which was highly doubtful given the sheer number of gryphons—all the gryphons had to do was tear the balloon, and the squirrel, beaver, and otter would find themselves floundering in the endless water. Even water mammals like a beaver and river otter need land to put their paws on eventually. And Witch-Hazel knew from experience she was a weak swimmer.

"What brings you to our island?" called out the closest gryphon—one with gray wings and gray tabby stripes—as it continued circling dizzyingly around the hot air balloon's basket.

Witch-Hazel hadn't seen the island yet, but now she spotted a jagged edge to the ocean in the distance. She wouldn't have recognized it as land yet, but it was the only part of the horizon, in any direction, that wasn't perfectly flat.

"Merry-Green the tortoise sent us. We're seeking her pen-pal, Occultus the octopus surgeon," Twiggy called back to the gryphon, teeth whistling nervously.

"I don't think you'd like what Occultus would do with mundane creatures like you," the gryphon cawed, coming in to land on the edge of their basket. "She'd make you less mundane. You probably wouldn't like the price you'd have to pay. Many of my fellows—" The gryphon gestured with a wing at the other gryphons, still circling, cawing, and meowing. "—their brains don't work the same after Occultus made them ... more magnificent."

The Otter's Wings

Witch-Hazel backed into the far side of the basket, and wished she had swords in her paws. Or maybe a magic spell to let her throw fireballs, since she seemed to always be without swords when she felt like she needed them.

The gryphon tilted its avian head and stared at Witch-Hazel with one of its wide golden eyes, seemingly completely aware of the small squirrel's violent feelings but also completely unfazed by them.

Up close, Witch-Hazel thought she could make out stitch-marks at the seams between the grypon's feathered head and wings and the furry body they were attached to. She'd grown almost entirely certain these gryphons were chimeras, sewn together from normal falcons and stray cats. And the suspicion made her even more doubtful about the idea of taking Fish-Breath to an octopus who increasingly sounded like a mad scientist. Still, they needed help from someone to heal his bleeding tail.

Fish-Breath dragged himself up from the floor of the basket and spread his tawny wings. They were larger and wider than the gryphon's slate gray ones. "I'm not mundane," the otter said. "Will you help us find Occultus?"

The gryphon's tabby striped tail twitched. Witch-Hazel found herself wondering what the gryphon's ears would be doing, if it had them. Avian expressions were so much harder to read for the lack of ears.

"Occultus will like you," the gryphon said. "You are magnificent already, and you'll give her new ideas. New inspiration." The gryphon flapped its wings and took flight again. "Follow us to the island, and we can give you a place to stow your balloon before sending you on your way down to Occultus's clinic."

"Thank you," Twiggy said.

Fish-Breath had already sunk back to the floor of the basket, a pile of tawny wings, brown fur, and short limbs, looking exhausted by his brief outburst of energy.

They couldn't get to a doctor too soon. Even a mad scientist doctor would be better than nothing.

7

THE JAGGED EDGE OF THE ISLAND resolved into a crescent as they approached—lined with a sandy beach on its outer curve, thickly forested in the middle, and rocky on the inner curve. It looked like the mostly submerged tip of an ancient volcano, grown over with thick flora and fauna.

The flock of gryphons guided Twiggy to steer the balloon towards the island's southernmost tip, where they landed on a flat plain between rocky outcroppings, above the tree line. Twiggy and Witch-Hazel sorted quickly through the supplies in the basket, dividing them into those to carry with them in packs and those to leave behind, stored with the folded up balloon.

Witch-Hazel made sure to pack the dried flower leis she'd made from air lilies, magical flowers that would allow her and Twiggy to breathe underwater if needed. Fish-Breath wouldn't need one, since he was granted endless breath by the moon opal encrusting his knuckle. But Witch-Hazel packed an extra lei anyway, just in case the octopus surgeon did manage to remove the Celestial Fragments from Fish-Breath, like he wanted.

Fish-Breath watched as they worked, making jokes to cover his discomfort over feeling too weak to help and useless because of it. Without needing to discuss it, Twiggy and Witch-Hazel packed only the lightest objects in Fish-Breath's pack, figuring his pack served more as a mental crutch for him at this point, so he wouldn't argue with them over babying him, and perhaps a useful bag to put things in later, if he got stronger. *When* he got stronger.

Surely, an otter imbued with magic from the sun, moon, and northern star couldn't be brought down by a single scrape from a shadowcat's claw. Occultus would know how to help him.

The whole time they were packing, Witch-Hazel was painfully aware of the gryphons, lazing about the plain, watching them with keen avian eyes and measuring the time impatiently with twitching feline tails. She also kept glancing at the shadows—those in the trees at the edge of the field and those thrown by large rocks—and wondering whether the shadowcats could find their way here. Worrying the shadowcats would climb out of those shadows, if they didn't move fast enough.

When the trio of travelers was ready to move on, Fish-Breath leaned against Twiggy for support, and Witch-Hazel took the lead, approaching the gryphon who had spoken to them before.

"Where do we go?" Witch-Hazel asked. "To get to Occultus's clinic?"

"I sent some of my little siblings to fetch Mother," the gryphon said, clacking its beak. "She's on her way. She'll carry you."

Witch-Hazel and Twiggy exchanged worried glances, but they didn't have time to wonder and fret too much about who "Mother" could be, before a much larger gryphon came flying over the rocky outcropping to the north of them.

This gryphon was fundamentally shaped like the others—avian head, wings, and talons sprouting from a feline body. But those disparate pieces didn't look cobbled together here; they flowed together with a wholeness that looked more than natural. It was supernatural. This was a true-born gryphon, a mythical creature, who belonged more among the ranks of the leontaur and unicorn who Witch-Hazel had encountered than with these tabby-falcons who looked like ethically questionable science experiments.

"This is Mother," the tabby gryphon meow-cawed as the much larger gryphon landed beside them.

"That's your name?" Witch-Hazel asked, trying to keep her voice from shaking, as she looked up at the giant creature standing before her. "Mother?"

"Yes," Mother said. Like the leontaur, her feline parts seemed to be leonine in nature. She had a lion's broad body, tufted tail, and giant back paws, all covered in fur gleaming golden in the late morning light. Her head, wings, and forelegs were covered in feathers as bright and sharp as cut copper, and her beak and talons looked like they could kill a squirrel effortlessly.

"Is it far?" Witch-Hazel asked bravely. "To the clinic?" She didn't want to draw attention to Fish-Breath's infirmity. Everything inside her screamed against showing vulnerability to a being like this one, but it wasn't like they could hide the otter's weakness. He could barely hold himself up. He wouldn't be able to walk far.

"You're all small," Mother said. "You may ride on my back, and I'll take you to my beloved's lair."

And so once again, Witch-Hazel found herself riding on a lion's back, listening to a mythical creature tell her stories, just as she had, so long ago, with the leontaur in the buried mole city. But this time, she wasn't alone, she had Fish-Breath in front of her, draped over the gryphon's feathered neck, and Twiggy behind her, perched on the gryphon's wide haunches. The gryphon had flared her wings a little, providing feathered railings to either side of her passengers. This was good, because Fish-Breath seemed too drained of energy from his ever-bleeding wound to balance himself without help.

Remembering her previous ride on the leonine back of a mythical creature, Witch-Hazel strained to focus on the nattering, meandering stories the gryphon told as she walked laconically across the plain, between the rocky outcroppings, and toward the inner curve of the crescent

The Otter's Wings

island. When the leontaur had told stories of the mole city, she'd expected Witch-Hazel to learn lessons from them and pass a test later. Of course, she'd been sister to the sphinx, and dealing in riddles and tricks was their way.

From listening to Mother, Witch-Hazel gathered gryphons were a wholly different kind of mythical creature, less singular and more part of a dwindling species. Grand, natural gryphons like Mother had once filled this island with their nests and intricate society, but over the span of Mother's long life, she'd watched her people die out, laying fewer and fewer eggs while even smaller numbers of those eggs ever hatched.

Mother was the last gryphon.

Until she met Occultus.

The octopus surgeon had sewn stray cats, rescued from the wreckage of a pirate ship, together with local falcons, making a brood of strange children for Mother to watch over and rule.

The fur along Witch-Hazel's spine prickled at the creepiness of Mother's story, but even more so over the creatures she saw hiding in rocky crags or shadowy shrubbery they passed.

Three headed mice. Snakes with mice legs all along their sides, making them into monstrous versions of centipedes. Tiny gryphons composed of mice and songbirds. And reverse gryphons with cat heads sprouting awkwardly out of avian shoulders, looking terribly unbalanced and slightly bewildered, as if their very own existence troubled them. Or perhaps, Witch-Hazel was projecting her feelings onto them ...

But given the reverse gryphons' flattened ears and blank stares, Witch-Hazel didn't think so. She remembered what the first tabby gryphon had told them about paying a price for magnificence and how not all of its fellow gryphons' brains worked right anymore.

Witch-Hazel didn't like the idea of handing Fish-Breath over to a knife-happy, mad scientist octopus, and she liked it less with everything she learned about Occultus's strange and upsetting hobby of shuffling the creatures on this island together like their body parts were a deck of cards, meant to be arranged and rearranged for the card player's entertainment.

The gryphon's path led over the crest of the island and down toward the lapping waves. As they approached, Witch-Hazel saw the curve of the island continued, under the clear blue water, curving further around, presumably completing the circle of this sunken volcano's mouth. The bright sunlight made Witch-Hazel feel warm and safe, as if the shadowcats must have been nothing more than a nightmare. But the bright sunlight also cast dark shadows, and each of them looked threatening.

The Otter's Wings

After navigating the rocky crags leading down to the beach, Mother took a sharp turn and headed into a round cave opening, filled with even more shadows.

The cave was so round and smooth, winding its way downward into the darkness; it had to be a lava tube. The bright daylight behind them dwindled with each padding footstep of Mother's paws and talons, but paler light twinkled ahead. Witch-Hazel expected the dull illumination to come from the flickering firelight of torches, but when they got to it, the lights reminded her more of an experimental glass bulb Twiggy had shown her once. Wires ran along the walls of the lava tube, connecting one bulb to the next. They had to be electric.

Witch-Hazel twisted around to catch Twiggy's expression: the beaver looked excited, her buck teeth bared in a wide grin. Between them, Fish-Breath looked engaged and curious. He enjoyed novelty. This island, so far, was overflowing with it. Witch-Hazel was pretty sure she didn't want to see any more novelty. She'd have liked a nice, familiar table at their favorite tavern in Riverton, followed by an evening of swinging in hammocks and staring at the stars.

Instead, Mother brought them to a wide cavern filled with tables covered with sharp tools, tangled bits of wire, and glass vessels of all shapes and sizes, mostly filled with brightly colored, frothy, bubbly liquids. Between the tables, there were iron cages, some of them inhabited by crazed, screeching chimerical animals, too jumbled together for Witch-Hazel to be sure where all their parts had come from. Though, one seemed to sport all the extra mouse tails that must have been left over from the three-headed mice and mouse-legged snakes outside. They'd been stuck into the creature, all over its body, like a thick, waving fur of cilia. Other creatures sported crablike pincers and legs, sprouting from furry bodies. All of it made Witch-Hazel shudder with horror.

Beyond the cages, there was a row of skeletons, one of each species of creature—the natural ones, not the chimeras—Witch-Hazel had seen on this island so far. They were arranged into a macabre display, like some kind of teaching device for a horrifying anatomy class. Behind the skeletons, a deep pool of water filled the rest of the cave, up to the far wall. The water looked like it extended down forever, probably deep enough to connect to the ocean.

The whole place was damp and dripping, each drop echoing and adding to the noise from the various chimeras, who seemed to be screaming and pointing at Mother and their new visitors.

Witch-Hazel didn't want to be a visitor here. She wanted to get herself and her friends out of here as fast as possible, before Occultus could decide to swap her and Twiggy's tails or maybe just sew all three of them into a three-headed monster.

Witch-Hazel loved her friends dearly, but she didn't want to be that close to them. She liked her own body, exactly as it was.

Though ... she supposed ... that's why they were here. Fish-Breath had liked his own body the way it had always been, without magical gemstones encrusting it and wings sprouting where they generally didn't belong. On an otter's back.

And at the very least, there had to be better supplies in this mad scientist's lair for healing Fish-Breath's tail than she and Twiggy had stowed away in their backpacks.

Witch-Hazel just hoped the shadowcats wouldn't be able to find them here. She didn't know what rules they followed, but the ocean had been a wide expanse of glittering brightness, without a shadow for them to step through, and they were cats after all. So, perhaps, by crossing those waters, Witch-Hazel's troupe had managed to leave the shadowcats behind.

Mother folded her wings down, and her passengers clambered off her back. Then the gryphon lifted a talon, pointed at a table clear of disturbing instruments, and said, "Lay the patient out there. Occultus will be here shortly."

With some trepidation, Witch-Hazel and Twiggy helped Fish-Breath up onto the table. His wings spread out behind him, their tips drooping over the table's edge on either side. Witch-Hazel climbed onto a stool beside the table, so she could see Fish-Breath better and took ahold of his closest paw, the one with the star sliver embedded in his wrist. Twiggy toddled around the room, looking at all the strange devices. She even stopped by several of the iron barred cages and seemed, fruitlessly, to try to talk to the chimeras trapped inside.

Witch-Hazel was gripped, suddenly, with a desire to free all the creatures from their cages and rampage through the rest of the clinic, breaking glass beakers and vials.

Instead, she squeezed Fish-Breath's paw with one hand, and grabbed onto his wrist with her other. She felt the sharp edges of the star sliver under her paw, and it helped her focus. She felt the tickle of static electricity in the gemstone, spreading warmth through her own paw, and once again, she felt her body grow lighter, like she had when Fish-Breath had been flying, carrying her through the sky. She looked down at her hind paws, almost expecting to find she was hovering over the surface of the stool, no longer touching it.

A slurping, slopping sound burbled up from the pool on the far side of the room, and instantly, every chimera fell silent. Eerily silent. The only sounds left were the echoing drops of water and a squishing, sucking noise caused by Occultus's tentacles pulling the octopus out of the water.

The tentacles were bright pink and wrinkly like the flesh of a torn-open watermelon, and they were smashed against the smooth rocky floor of the cavern as if gravity pressed down harder on them than on creatures with skeletons or exoskeletons. Nevertheless, the pink flesh flexed and strained and pulled itself up onto the relatively dry surface of the rock, revealing a bulbous body and two eerie blobs with eyes in them attached to the nexus at the middle of the tentacles.

Witch-Hazel was wondering how such a squashed-down creature expected to operate on a table so far above the ground when Occultus surprised her—instead of continuing to squish her way along the floor, the octopus crawled her slippery, sinewy way up into the nearest animal skeleton on display. She climbed inside the gleaming white rib cage of a long deceased creature—from its long spine and relatively shorter limbs, Witch-Hazel though it might have been an otter; it was certainly about the same size as Fish-Breath.

Occultus filled the skeleton's ribcage with her bulbous body, and her eyes stared out, pale as the bones around them and twice as unnerving. She wrapped a pink tentacle around each skeletal limb, filling them out and becoming the muscle they no longer had. She wore the skeleton like an exoskeleton and worked the legs with four tentacles, making the whole thing lurch unnervingly as it walked across the cavern, up to the table where Fish-Breath was laid out, waiting to be tended to … or perhaps filleted.

Occultus's remaining four tentacles—that weren't busy working the legs—reached out of the rib cage and began moving in complicated patterns, their slender tips twisting and coiling as if in a dance. The skeleton's skull perched atop the body constructed of dead bones and living octopus flesh, a totally unnecessary decoration that bobbled about with Occultus's every move. Its jaw chattered like a death rattle.

Mother stepped forward, placing herself across the table from Occultus and said, "Octopuses don't have voices like us. They speak in sign language." Then she placed a small cage on the corner of the table, beside Fish-Breath's head, and opened its door. A small yellow songbird with black and white checkmarks on her wingtips and head hopped out. "This bird's name and role is Voice," Mother said. "It will translate."

Witch-Hazel noted the bitter irony of the fact that Occultus had torn apart every other creature in this den of torture and sewn them back together at her whim ... except for the songbird. Occultus relied on a natural creature, uncontaminated by her knife and needle to play the part of her voice.

The songbird's voice rose in a lilting trill to say, "Welcome to my clinic. I understand, from what my children have told me, you are sent by my longtime friend Merry-Green. Is the tortoise well?" The bird's voice was beautiful, but also haunting, filled with a hollowness, like

The Otter's Wings

the bird spoke the words she had to, but tried her best to keep her mind uninvolved.

Witch-Hazel wondered where the songbird's mind wandered to while translating for Occultus.

Twiggy drew a whistling breath through her buck teeth and said, "Merry-Green is as well as ever. She said you might help us—our friend here, he's dependent on these magical gems—" Twiggy pointed with blunt, shovel-like claws at the gems on his chest, wrist, and knuckle. "—the Celestial Fragments, to keep him alive. They've given him wings. But he doesn't want the wings. He doesn't want the gems. Can you remove them? Without hurting him?"

Fish-Breath sighed deeply as his friend spoke for him, as if each word took a weight off his shoulders.

"And his tail," Witch-Hazel added. "There's a wound on his tail that won't stop bleeding. Can you do anything for that?"

Occultus's tentacle tips wriggled, and Voice sang, "I will examine him." Then the four tentacles played over Fish-Breath's body, running up and down his long otter torso, short limbs, and broad wings, touching him everywhere but paying especial attention to where the Celestial Fragments were embedded.

8

The whole time Occultus spent examining Fish-Breath, Witch-Hazel spent examining their surroundings, letting her gaze pass methodically over every surface, every nook and cranny, and every shadow in the room. She didn't move, not wanting to draw attention to herself or her activity, but she made plans in her mind, identifying sharp tools that looked like she might be able to reach them before the octopus or gryphon could catch her and mapping out what path would get her back to the lava tube leading to the surface fastest. She wanted to be ready to guide and defend her friends out of here, even under duress, if it came to that.

Occultus's tentacles stopped roving over Fish-Breath's body, held still for a long moment, and then two of them coiled back toward the rib cage holding the rest of the octopus, like two arms folding across her chest. Except the arms were tentacles, covered in sucker discs and tapering down to mere threads at their ends, and the chest was bare bones filled with pulsating, gleaming, pink flesh and two pale eyes.

Occultus's other two tentacles traced out a complicated glyph in the air, and Voice sang, "You want the patient to live, yes?"

"Yes!" Twiggy and Witch-Hazel shouted at the same time.

"And keep his original brain? I have many other fine brains that could be used to reanimate him if he didn't survive at first."

Fish-Breath sighed even more deeply, as if these questions had already told him the news he'd feared and expected. Occultus couldn't help him.

Twiggy said firmly, "That will not do. We need him to keep the same brain."

Witch-Hazel was too angry to form words.

"Just asking," Voice translated, as Occultus's tentacles continued dancing in the air. "No need to get upset." The songbird's voice stayed emotionless, but the movement of the tentacles—now rejoined by the two that had folded across the chest of the skeleton—took on a frenzied tone in their movements. "There are many things I could do with a specimen as magnificent as this one—"

There was that word again. Magnificent. Witch-Hazel cut the songbird's translations off, snapping, "We don't want many things. We only want two—remove the gemstones and wings, and *heal his tail!* If you can't do those, then—"

The Otter's Wings

"Stop," Twiggy said. The beaver had waddled up beside the stool where Witch-Hazel was perched and laid a heavy paw on the squirrel's shoulder. "We need to listen."

Words frothed just inside Witch-Hazel's mouth—words like "lunatic" and "madness," "evil" and "abhorrent"—but she snapped her mouth shut, and kept the barbed words safely behind her sharp teeth. They had come a long way. The octopus wasn't holding any knives in her tentacles yet. She could afford to listen.

Twiggy turned to the octopus, still keeping her paw firmly on Witch-Hazel's shoulder, and said, "What can you do for our friend, without damaging his … uh … current form? And what about the wound on his tail? Can you heal it?"

Occultus's pink flesh blanched white and then blushed through several shades of blues and purple before returning to the bright, raw color of the inside of a watermelon. She ran her tentacles, three of them, over Fish-Breath's tail, lifted the thick rudder-like appendage gently, and moved it from side to side. Then she unwrapped the layers of blood soaked bandages, revealing the soggy, matted fur underneath. Still wet with fresh blood.

The barbed words held inside Witch-Hazel's mouth turned venomous as she realized Occultus hadn't even bothered examining the wound on Fish-Breath's tail until now. The octopus scientist had been too interested in chopping him up and sewing him into one of her zombie chimeras to pay attention to the idea of any actual healing. But Twiggy's paw on Witch-Hazel's shoulder steadied her, and she managed to hold her tongue.

"This wound is supernatural," Voice sang. Occultus still held Fish-Breath's injured tail with three tentacles, but the fourth one reached out of the skeletal rib cage and contorted in complex configurations, apparently able to communicate through sign language all on its own.

Occultus laid down Fish-Breath's tail and—Witch-Hazel gasped to see—pulled open a small drawer under the table, filled with knives. The squirrel's paws tightened into fists, and her entire body tensed, ready leap across the table and wrestle an octopus several times her size and far more flexible than her for whatever sharp implement might shortly menace her friend.

But Occultus didn't grab a knife. She wrapped the tip of her tentacle firmly around a small brown bottle. "This is coagulant," Voice sang as two of Occultus's tentacles danced in sign language and the other two un-stoppered the bottle. "It will help the wound stop bleeding and begin to heal. Then I can sew it shut."

Witch-Hazel relaxed and watched the octopus pour a fine grained, mustard yellow powder on Fish-Breath's tail. Occultus closed the bottle and put it back in the drawer, while at the same time massaging the powder into Fish-Breath's wound. The yellow powder turned crusty and then disappeared into his thick, wet fur.

The Otter's Wings

Next Occultus picked out a needle and thread from the drawer, using tentacle tips almost as narrow as the needle itself. She worked so carefully, so precisely with her tentacles that even Witch-Hazel—who had been biased against the octopus from the beginning and disliked nearly everything about her—couldn't help being impressed. The needle flashed as it jumped up and down, in and out of Fish-Breath's fur, under the deft guidance of Occultus's tentacles. The otter held preternaturally still, perhaps afraid of messing up the octopus's work. Or perhaps, the blood loss was really getting to him. He had been unusually quiet since entering Occultus's lair. It pained Witch-Hazel to see such a usually loquacious, cheerful otter brought so low.

The work was done in a matter of moments, and Occultus pulled the loose thread under the base of her arms, inside the skeletal rib cage, where she bit it off with her tiny, sharp, hidden beak.

Witch-Hazel laughed in spite of herself, and everyone in the room turned to stare at her with daunting eyes. "I'm sorry," Witch-Hazel chittered, "I was just struck by the strangeness ... you're so different—" She gestured at Occultus and Mother. "—and yet you both have beaks. All those differences, wings, tentacles, fur, feathers, and color-changing skin covered in suction discs. And yet, under it all, you have the same kind of mouth."

Mother titled her eagle head, and Occultus's skin flushed through several shades of yellow, matching different parts of her gryphon partner's body—the gold of a lion's fur, the copper of her feathers, and the plain, serviceable yellow of her beak and talons. Then the skin around the octopus's pale eyes crinkled, and she spoke through her tentacles to say with her proxy Voice, "Yes, deep inside we all have hearts beating, moving blood through our bodies. We are all machines processing the chaos of the natural world into a brief spark called life. We are more the same inside than it seems on the surface."

For a moment, Witch-Hazel looked at Occultus and instead of seeing a horrifying monster who chopped apart innocent animals for entertainment ... she saw an aspect of the All-Being reflected in those tentacles and in the way the octopus desired to bring all these creatures together, even when those combinations seemed unnatural to her.

The way the All-Being had reflected every living animal on Earth, flowing from one form into the next—growing legs and shedding wings, trading one body type for another like an image tumbling in a kaleidoscope—wasn't so different from what Occultus seemed to be trying to capture here.

Occultus's skin returned to the glaring shade of watermelon pink she seemed to be most comfortable with, and Voice translated her signing, "The physical aspects of this wound will heal now, but the supernatural aspects ...

The Otter's Wings

I cannot heal those. I am a scientist, not a magician. Now as for the wings and gemstones—obviously, I can remove them."

Fish-Breath shifted on the table, turning his head so he could look at the octopus, his eyes filled with hope.

Voice continued singing: "The recovery from having the wings removed might be long and painful, but there's no question the patient would survive. They're physical, biological components of his body, and removing them would be a simple surgery. The Celestial Fragments, however, are magical. They have a supernatural component, and so while I can easily remove them, I cannot guarantee how the host's body would respond. Can you tell me more about them? If so, perhaps I could give you a better idea of what to expect from their removal."

"How long?" Fish-Breath asked. "How long would the recovery be from removing the wings?"

A single wiggle of a single tentacle tip led to Voice singing, "Months. At least."

Twiggy's paw, still resting on Witch-Hazel's shoulder squeezed, and the squirrel turned to see the beaver staring intently at her, tilting her head, implying they should confer more privately.

"Can we have a minute?" Witch-Hazel asked.

Mother's feathers puffed out irritably, and Occultus's skin flushed through a rainbow of colors, while her tentacles signed frantically.

"You came to me," Voice sang, mechanically, entirely failing to mirror the inscrutable emotions flooding the octopus's expressive body. "You have already taken many minutes of my time, with no warning, no offer of recompense, and very little of the respect I am due. Instead, you have barged into our haven on this island—*our home*—and behaved judgmentally, laughing at our physical differences and implying with your every movement and gesture that my work here—designed to build a family for myself and my beloved—makes me some kind of heretical monster and our life together unnatural."

"I didn't say—" Witch-Hazel began, but the bird's mechanical singing rushed on.

"You didn't have to *say*. You have exuded disdain and derision with every tilt of your head, flick of your tail, and flattening of your ears."

Mother spoke in a low, growly voice: "Octopuses are masters of nonverbal communication. They need to be. And our mammalian reflexes and gestures are painfully simple in comparison to the language of their bodies. We are easy to read."

"You are lucky I am considering your case at all," Voice sang. "Instead of exiling you back to the open ocean. Now tell me about these Celestial Fragments." Occultus folded all four of her free tentacles over the skeletal rib cage encasing her body, just below her piercing, pale eyes.

The Otter's Wings

Her skin had faded to the same pale color of her eyes and the bleached bones she wore like armor. She looked furious.

In a confused way, Witch-Hazel felt abashed. She had been judging this octopus and gryphon from the moment she'd met each of them. And yet …

"The tabby gryphon who guided us to your island …" Witch-Hazel said, knowing she might be signing a death warrant for all of them, but finding herself seemingly unable to stopper the words in her mouth from tumbling out anymore. "It said many of the other gryphons you'd made didn't … I don't remember exactly, but their brains weren't right anymore after you'd altered them." She fumbled to a stop.

Mother sighed deeply and muttered, "Cassio."

"What?" Witch-Hazel asked, feeling confused, scared, and frankly like she wished to be anywhere else but here, doing anything else but talking to this octopus and gryphon.

"Cassio is a troublemaker," Mother said. "She was trying to scare you. Certainly, you've heard of cats being troublemakers before? Well, some gryphons are too. We are half cat, after all."

"What?" Witch-Hazel repeated. "So … it was a lie?"

"Not exactly," Voice sang as Occultus's tentacles began dancing again. "Sometimes I try to save animals who've injured themselves. Sometimes I am … too late to save them entirely. But I never perform surgeries on those of intellect without consent, so long as the patient or their guardian is capable of providing such."

Witch-Hazel felt like Occultus's statement held too many qualifiers to be truly comforting, but she lost interest in the octopus's words as Fish-Breath sat up on the table. The otter folded his wings tightly against his back, and swung his feet down to the floor. Everyone in the room watched him as he wobbled uncertainly, then walked about, looking at various caged chimeras.

Witch-Hazel hadn't been certain he was still strong enough to stand.

"I don't know," Fish-Breath said, "if I can afford to spend months recovering ... not with the shadowcats ..." He trailed off, distracted by all the strange—wonderful and horrible—curiosities around him.

Everyone else stayed silent, practically holding their breaths, waiting for him to continue speaking. But instead, the otter explored—he liked novelty—and placed his paws on everything he saw, gently touching iron bars and corners of tables. Partly, he seemed to be seeking physical support, as he was still weak, but he also seemed to be trying to understand this place through touch, letting it sink into even more of his senses. Finally, he came to a large speckled egg in a nest of woven twigs, set on a stony pedestal. He laid his webbed paws on the egg's surface and said, "It's warm."

Now it was Mother's turn to say, "What?"

The Otter's Wings

"Warm," Fish-Breath repeated. "What kind of egg is it?"

"Ours," Voice sang.

Everyone except Mother turned to look at Occultus.

Mother kept staring at the egg.

Occultus's tentacles danced, and Voice explained, "Mother and I have been trying to create a true natural hybrid child for ourselves. I surgically combine the eggs I lay with her eggs while they're still developing, and … They never hatch."

"They're never warm." Mother's voice had turned husky with emotion.

Voice's singing stayed emotionless, but Occultus's skin flushed every color of the rainbow.

The egg under Fish-Breath's paws—his Celestial Fragment encrusted paws—began to crack.

9

Witch-Hazel smelled the friable scent of ozone in the air, and her view of the egg under Fish-Breath's paws waved like a mirage in the desert. Was he channeling Celestial magic into the egg? Bringing it to life? Helping it to hatch? She wasn't sure, but for sure, it did hatch.

Fragments of shell wiggled and burst outward, followed by tiny pink tentacles, wriggling and writhing through the gaps left behind. Mother rushed to the side of the egg, her copper wings lifting off her back into a half-mast position. Occultus rattled her way across the room to stand by the gryphon's side, still wearing her otter-like skeleton.

The two strange creatures, both mothers of this egg, waited nervously, watching as the tiny pink tentacles broke off more fragments of shell, widening the gap, until a strange baby was revealed inside: pink tentacles fringed the creature's face, like a prehensile beard under a yellow beak and pale eyes. Its body was a mess of golden feathers and pink skin, like some kind of infantile version of an elder god, the sight of which should drive sane creatures mad.

Mother lifted up one of her talons, and Occultus wrapped a tentacle tightly around it as they both stared wide-eyed at their new child.

"This egg should have hatched days ago," Mother choked out in a rough voice. "We had given up hope."

Occultus's free tentacles danced, and Voice sang; for once, a note of brightness and cheer entered the bird's song. "I can't understand this at all. I examined the egg this morning, and the heartbeat inside was too weak ... much too weak to survive hatching. It should have died. And yet ... this miracle has happened. The magic in those gemstones ..."

"It's very powerful," Fish-Breath said, finishing the octopus's thought. The words sounded like a realization as he said them. A sad yet reverent realization. "You can't remove them from me. No one can."

"No, I cannot," Occultus agreed. "I wouldn't dare try. Not now."

Fish-Breath's wings drooped until the tawny feather tips dragged on the stone floor. "Not even the wings?"

"They're part and parcel of the Celestial Fragments' magic, aren't they?" Occultus asked through Voice.

Fish-Breath didn't answer. He didn't have to. Instead, he said, "We came all this way. And you were our only hope."

Witch-Hazel wasn't about to argue with her beloved otter as he mourned his own hope dying, but she still harbored other hopes. She hoped he would accept his wings and the gift of the Celestial Fragments, and they could stop seeking a solution he didn't really need.

They could go back to Riverton, and stare at the starry sky while lying in hammocks at night. They could sit by the river during the heat of day, trailing their hind paws in the cool water, and laugh together. They could make leaf houses and throw acorns at the tavern while waiting for the chef to fry up the fish Fish-Breath had caught during the day.

They could take a break from adventuring.

Of course, none of that was possible as long as the shadowcats were chasing them.

In a rush, Witch-Hazel decided it was time to trust Occultus and Mother with everything they knew about the Celestial Fragments. She'd been holding back—and suspected Twiggy and Fish-Breath had been doing the same—because she was afraid Occultus might try to cut the gems out of Fish-Breath's body and keep them for herself. Who knew what wonders and horrors this mad scientist octopus could concoct with the mix of magic and science that would become possible if she had possession of the Celestial Fragments?

But now the octopus was afraid and awed by their power. And indebted to Fish-Breath for the miracle he had unwittingly performed. Not to mention distracted by her sudden motherhood.

Witch-Hazel spoke before she could change her mind: "The gemstones are pieces of the Sun, the Moon, and the North Star. The Mouse King of the Earthen Realm broke them off, hoping to claim their magic for himself. Something must have gone wrong, and they were lost deep under the earth in a labyrinth."

"Where we found them," Fish-Breath added.

"And used them to save his life," Twiggy said, gesturing at their otter friend.

Witch-Hazel continued the story: "Now magic is leaking out of the cracks where the gemstones were taken, draining magic out of the world, which is probably why the gryphons are dying out, and also, there are these shadows ..."

"Shadowcats," Twiggy said.

"Yes, shadowcats chasing Fish-Breath," Witch-Hazel said. "One of them caused the wound in his tail. I don't know *if* or *how* they're related to the gemstones, but I think the shadowcats want them. They lost our trail when our balloon flew over the ocean. But ..." Witch-Hazel looked around the shadowy cavern and shuddered. There were shadows everywhere in here.

"But you may have led them to our home." Mother's voice had gone hollow, and Occultus's skin had flushed as pale as her eyes.

"We're sorry," Witch-Hazel said. "And we'll leave ... but ... we don't know where to go. Or who could help us.

The Otter's Wings

Do you ... have any ideas? Any suggestions of where else we might find help?"

"You have to go to the Mouse King," Mother said. "He caused this. He will solve it."

Witch-Hazel wasn't sure she wanted to know what kind of solution the Mouse King might provide. And yet, she had no better idea.

Occultus recovered a faint, petal-pink version of her usual coloring and began signing. Voice sang, "From the mythology I've studied of the elements and their royal stewards, the shadowcats are most likely minions of the Mouse King. Even if you could work the miracle of finding him—a mythical figure from the distant past—he'd be unlikely to be your ally."

Witch-Hazel had met enough mythical figures from the distant past that she wasn't daunted by the prospect. But she agreed with Occultus's concerns as to what the Mouse King's motives might be if they found him.

When they found him. If he'd sent the shadowcats to chase Fish-Breath, then they had no choice but to find him. It was either that or run from the shadowcats for the rest of their days. And Witch-Hazel didn't like their prospects, as far as hiding from the king of an entire realm was concerned.

"So ... how do we find him?" Twiggy asked.

Occultus answered through Voice, "A possibly fictional figure from dim, dusty, and ancient mythology?

That is not my area of expertise. I am a scientist and doctor, not a conjurer of legends."

Witch-Hazel found Occultus's statement vaguely ridiculous as the octopus's consort, the last gryphon, was herself a figure from legend who most of the animals in Riverton would have considered part of Fish-Breath's unbelievable tall tales and not someone who could actually be met and talked to ... Like so many of the creatures who Witch-Hazel had spent adventures meeting and talking to.

Even so, the octopus was right: she wasn't an expert on conjuring royal stewards of the elemental realms.

Whereas, arguably, Witch-Hazel was. She had met Amalah, salamander queen of the Fire Realm; Kokeu, koi queen of the Water Realm; and Mercy, butterfly queen of the Air Realm all in person. In fact, she had even given Mercy her name.

There was no one in the world likely to know more about how to find the mouse king than herself. So Witch-Hazel strained to remember every detail about how she'd met the three queens, anything that might help her here. However, her remembrance was interrupted by Mother scraping her talons across the rock floor, creating a horrible, shrill shriek, and crying out in her hoarse husky voice, "You must go! You tell us you may have led trouble to our doorstep? And yet you linger here? Occultus has answered you: we cannot help! So, you must leave before leading these dangerous shadows into our home!"

Abashed, Fish-Breath lowered his webbed paw from where he'd been tickling the baby elder god under its tentacles, causing them to blush pink and yellow like a tiny sunrise. "Mother is right," he said. "The shadowcats are chasing me. We shouldn't stay in one place long enough for them to find us." The otter turned to the skeleton-garbed octopus and bowed deeply, "Thank you for healing my tail."

The songbird, Voice, fluttered off the table beside Fish-Breath and flew across the cavern to perch on the pedestal holding the newly hatched egg. She spread her yellow wings, holding them in front of the baby's tentacled face, and the gryphon-octopus hybrid changed color as if its flesh were a mirror, reflecting the yellow wings as well as the black-and-white checkered pattern along Voice's wingtips.

Voice closed her wings, tilted her head, and then opened her wings again to take flight. This time, she landed on the wide, flat shoulder bone of Occultus's skeleton garb. She twittered softly, singing words too quiet for anyone but the octopus beside her to hear. Occultus's skin darkened as Voice whisper-sang, until the writhing tentacles filling out the bleached bones of the otter skeleton had grown the dark purple of a bruised, overripe plum.

Witch-Hazel was deeply curious about the bird and octopus's conversation, but Mother growled like a lioness ready to defend her newborn cub and the squirrel found herself being dragged toward the entrance to the cavern by both of her friends. Twiggy and Fish-Breath clearly didn't want to tangle with Mother, and while Witch-Hazel could respect that—she also didn't want to fight a gryphon large enough for the three of them to ride—she felt like something important was happening, and she didn't want to miss it.

"Come on," Twiggy urged. "We need to get back to the balloon."

"If we're done here," Fish-Breath added, "we're safer in the air over the open ocean than around all these shadows." The otter glanced about nervously. He clearly didn't want to face the shadowcats again. He didn't want another wound that wouldn't heal.

"Wait!" Voice sang from behind them. The small songbird flew past them, a fluttering ball of feathers, and landed on the cavern floor at their feet. "Bring me with you."

"What?" Witch-Hazel asked, agape.

All the cheer and brightness that had been lacking from the bird's voice earlier filled it now as she rushed through her song-like story: "I've more than worked off my payment to Occultus for rescuing my hatch-mate when his neck broke. Long-Feather loves being a gryphon,

The Otter's Wings

and he's happy with the others. It was worth the work I've done as Occultus's translator to give him that. But I'm ready to leave, and I long for adventures, and, and, and … I know things! Lots of things! I've been working here for so long, and I learn everything Occultus learns. I've been at her side for years. I'm sure I could help you somehow."

The squirrel, beaver, and winged otter stared at the bright yellow bird at their feet wordlessly.

"Please!" she sang again. "Please let me come!"

Suddenly, the bird reminded Witch-Hazel of herself, when she'd first joined Twiggy and Fish-Breath. But also of Zwi, who was also yellow and black, though much smaller, when she'd joined their party. And even of Mercy, the baby caterpillar who'd grown into a moth-butterfly and then a full-fledged god under her care. Their adventuring party had grown and shrunk during her travels. Maybe it was time for it to grow again.

"Of course you can come," Witch-Hazel said, answering for all of them. Neither Twiggy nor Fish-Breath objected. Witch-Hazel wasn't sure whether they were deferring to her decision, or simply agreed with her choice. Either way, the songbird fluttered her wings happily, hopping from the floor of the cavern up to hover at the height of Witch-Hazel's pointed ears.

"Thank you! Thank you!" she said, wings flapping rapidly. "You won't regret it."

"Fine," Twiggy grumbled. Her tone suggested less that she agreed with Witch-Hazel and more that she knew better than to argue with the spirited squirrel over a choice like this. "But get moving, Voice. We need to move fast."

"Dappled-Sun," the bird corrected.

"What's that?" Fish-Breath asked.

"My name is Dappled-Sun, not Voice. Not anymore, now that I'm leaving, I'm back to the name I hatched to."

"Charming," Twiggy said. Then she grabbed Fish-Breath by the paw and yanked him with her into the tunnel. "Now, *come on.*"

Witch-Hazel scurried after them, and Dappled-Sun flew along beside her. The shadows dancing on the cave walls menaced the small group, but only in the normal way of shadows. None of them formed into the shape of cats. None of them clawed at Fish-Breath.

And finally, the sunlight of the island outside reached through the distant mouth of the tunnel, promising escape and a clear path to Twiggy's hot air balloon.

But not soon enough.

10

THE LIGHT AT THE END of the tunnel flickered and faded, like the shadow of a tree had moved as its branches swayed in a breeze, blocking the light. But the shadow didn't sway away. It resolved, sharpening around the edges, until three shadowcats stood at the mouth of the tunnel, ears perked up and tails held high. They were the gray of shadows cast by the moon at midnight.

Twiggy and Fish-Breath stopped running. Witch-Hazel almost crashed into the beaver's back, and Dappled-Sun fluttered higher, up to the ceiling of the tunnel to avoid slamming into Fish-Breath.

"What do we do?" Fish-Breath asked. He stepped backward. "I can't face them."

Witch-Hazel's paws itched for swords. She wished she'd grabbed one of the surgical knives she'd seen lying around in Occultus's clinic. Stealing from the mad scientist octopus probably wouldn't have been a good idea, but it certainly seemed like a better idea than facing these shadowcats empty pawed. The group had no chance at fighting them here, in the tunnel, with no weapons.

"We go back," Witch-Hazel said. "There are weapons in Occultus's lab."

"But there's no way out of that cavern!" Twiggy exclaimed. "We'll be backing ourselves into a corner!"

"We're already backed into a corner," Witch-Hazel hissed.

"Wait," Dappled-Sun whistled, still fluttering above their heads. "That's not true—Occultus's pool of water leads to the open ocean."

All three furry mammals turned to stare up at the little bird.

"Is that true?" Witch-Hazel's heart was beating so fast, she could hardly think.

"Yes, but it's long and winding. Occultus has been working on crafting breathing masks, but—"

Witch-Hazel cut off the bird, speaking directly to Fish-Breath, who could breathe underwater due to the endless breath granted by the Moon Opal encrusting his knuckle: "Run back, dive in the water, and swim out as fast as you can."

"But—" Fish-Breath tried to object, but Witch-Hazel grabbed his free paw, shaking her head both furiously and sadly. Twiggy was still holding tight to the other one.

"They're chasing you," Witch-Hazel said. "They'll ignore us. We can get to the balloon. We'll meet you on the open ocean when you surface."

The Otter's Wings

Fish-Breath glanced frantically at Twiggy, looking for an ally. He didn't seem to like the idea of parting ways any better than Witch-Hazel liked suggesting it. She had traveled so far and worked so hard to rejoin him after he'd ascended to the All-Being's castle in the sky. She was loathe to ever let him out of her sight again. Especially now. But it was the only way.

Twiggy said, "She's right. The shadowcats won't bother us. At least, they didn't bother me before, when you flew on ahead. This is our only chance. Neither of us is as strong of a swimmer as you. Even me. We'd only slow you down."

"I don't want to go alone," Fish-Breath complained. His rudder-like tail had begun swaying nervously, like he was anticipating another cold shadowcat's paw slashing against it.

Witch-Hazel twisted around and pulled one of her air lily leis out of her backpack. "Here," she said, thrusting it upward at Dappled-Sun. "Wear this and grab onto Fish-Breath's shoulder. It'll let you breathe underwater, and you're small enough he can bring you with him without being slowed down." She wished she could be the one to go with Fish-Breath instead, but this was the smart choice. She hated having to make the smart choice.

With a solemn nod agreeing to the plan, Fish-Breath grabbed the lei from Witch-Hazel's paws and took off running. Dappled-Sun fluttered after him.

Witch-Hazel and Twiggy found themselves standing alone in a lava tube, waiting for three dangerous shadows to advance on them. "Is there anything we can do ... to slow them down?" Witch-Hazel asked, uncertainly. She tried to think of everything in her backpack, trying to imagine how any of it could be used to delay the shadowcats, but it was mostly food and air lily leis. Useless.

"I have an artificial torch in my pack," Twiggy said. "But if light stopped them ..."

The beaver didn't have to finish the thought. Light cast shadows, and the shadowcats didn't seem bothered by light unless there was simply so much of it that there wasn't room left for shadows. An artificial torch wouldn't help.

"Then the best thing we can do is get to the balloon quickly," Witch-Hazel whispered, steeling herself to run down the end of the passage, past the shadowcats. "Follow me, and try not to let them touch you."

"Wait," Twiggy said. "The torch might not slow them down, but it could help us keep the shadowcats from touching us. Twiggy pulled the gadget out of her backpack, flicked a switch on its shaft, and the end lit up with an artificially steady glow. The beaver held it forward like a sword, and then she took off at a waddling run. Witch-Hazel scurried beside her, keeping close, and matching her pace to the larger, slower gait of her friend.

The Otter's Wings

The beaver and squirrel squeezed close to each other as the shadowcats rushed past them, like a cold wind, chilling their noses, tickling their whiskers, and rustling their fur. The echoing sounds of the tunnel seemed to dampen in the darkness of the shadowcats.

And then, like a dream disappearing when you wake up, all three shadowcats were gone, behind them, disappearing down the tunnel, chasing after Fish-Breath and Dappled-Sun.

Witch-Hazel's heart ached that this songbird who they'd only just met got to cling to Fish-Breath's thick fur and stay beside him, knowing whether he was safe or dying. And she had to run the other way. She had to stay with Twiggy. She had to climb over the rocks Mother had navigated so easily with her long leonine legs and large paws. She had to return to the folded up hot air balloon and help Twiggy spread the colorful cloth out, rev the engine that poured hot air upward, and hold the mouth of the balloon open while the air slowly—oh so slowly, how could it be so slow? didn't it know she was in a hurry?—filled the balloon up.

The hot air balloon's basket tottered on the sandy ground as the balloon itself filled enough to begin pulling the entire contraption off the ground.

Witch-Hazel's body lifted off the ground with the hot air balloon, and her fur nearly crackled with the heat from the midday sunlight beating down on the Isle of Gryffindell.

But her mind was underground, maybe even underwater, with Fish-Breath, and her heart was frozen as cold as the air chilled by the presence of the shadowcats. Her whole body clenched with the pain of being away from him and the fear he'd never resurface in the ocean. He'd die, slashed every which way, by the cold paws of the shadowcats, deep under Occultus's lair. And Witch-Hazel would never see him again.

She couldn't know that version of reality wasn't true until she saw him again. And she didn't know how to keep breathing, waiting for that moment to come—the moment when she spotted him in the bright glare of ocean water stretching out below them. He had to resurface. He had to escape the shadowcats. He had to survive. All of this—all of her adventures, everything she'd accomplished and become—would be hollow without him.

Witch-Hazel had thought it was hard waiting for Twiggy's balloon to appear in the distance when she'd been held close against Fish-Breath's chest and he'd been flying away from the first shadowcat. This was so much harder. She was perfectly safe, standing in the hot air balloon's basket above the wide, sparkling ocean, surrounded by packs of food and supplies, with one of her friends beside her, and yet her heart was somewhere down there, under the crashing waves, vulnerable and pursued by dark forces.

The Otter's Wings

Witch-Hazel locked her eyes on the part of the ocean in the leeward curve of the island, where she guessed Fish-Breath was most likely to surface.

Chimerical gryphons flew through the clouds around the balloon, keeping a polite distance, and whenever one of their shadows flickered over the water beneath, Witch-Hazel's heart jumped, trying to turn the shadow into Fish-Breath.

"Look," Twiggy said, touching Witch-Hazel's tense shoulder lightly. The beaver was pointing at the rocky side of the island, near the lava tube down to Occultus's lair.

The shadows between the rocks moved, prowling restlessly. Uncertain. Unhappy. Failed in their task …

"Fish-Breath made it into the underwater tunnel," Witch-Hazel said, wonderingly. "He must have. Or the shadowcats would still be down there."

"They must not be able to follow him into the water," Twiggy said, "any more than they seem to be able to follow our balloon over the wide open ocean."

Witch-Hazel shook her head. "They got to the island somehow. I wish I knew how. I think …" She frowned. "I think it's important."

"To know how our enemy can travel? Yeah," Twiggy agreed, "That does seem important."

"Our enemy," Witch-Hazel repeated the words, hardly able to make sense of them.

In all of her travels and adventures, Witch-Hazel had been drawn into many battles, many fights, but she'd never had an enemy pursue her before. True, the snake who'd sent her on the quest to find the lost Celestial Fragments in the first place had been manipulating her and turned on her after she'd found them. But from her point of view, the snake hadn't seemed like her enemy until the final battle began.

She'd never had an enemy chase her, continuing their antipathy across many days and great distances. Yet now—even though the shadowcats were technically pursuing Fish-Breath and not her—she had an enemy.

And she realized, they really were *her enemy.* Not just Fish-Breath's pursuers. They had hurt her friend and were trying to claim something that belonged to her—because regardless of Fish-Breath, she was the one who'd found the Celestial Fragments. She was the one who'd placed them on Fish-Breath's chest, wrist, and finger to save him. She was the one who'd brought them, encrusted on her best friend's body, back down from the All-Being's castle in the sky.

The Celestial Fragments belonged to her, and if those shadowcats would hurt her friend in pursuit of them, then they were her enemy. And whether Fish-Breath ever surfaced or not *(he had to surface, he really had to, and he could breathe forever down there, so if all three shadowcats were prowling uselessly around the island, then he was safe and would emerge when he was ready)* Witch-Hazel would have to reckon with the shadowcats. Whatever they wanted the Celestia Fragments for … she needed to find that out, and she needed to stop them.

"The Mouse King," Witch-Hazel said. "Occultus thought the shadowcats must work for the Mouse King, right?"

"Yeah," Twiggy agreed, still staring down at the ocean, while second-naturedly tugging the ropes steering the hot air balloon, holding it steady above the island's cove.

"Then the Mouse King is our enemy, and we need to stop him." The squirrel's words came from between gritted teeth, low and quiet.

Twiggy most likely missed them, covered by the distant caws of the gryphons and the gentle sighing of the salty wind. Either way, she didn't respond. Instead, she sobbed in relief, saying, "There he is!"

By the time Witch-Hazel caught sight of Fish-Breath, he was already out of the water, flying toward them, Dappled-Sun fluttering along beside him. Droplets of salt water streamed off his feathers, sprinkling back down to the sea he'd emerged from in a glittering rainbow.

The otter crashed into the basket, tumbling to the floor in an exhausted yet also comically acrobatic somersault. He was still a clown at heart, in spite of everything he'd gone through. The songbird, however, landed primly on the basket's edge and shook the excess water out of her wings. She'd had to wrap the air lily lei around herself three times to make it tight enough to stay on.

Twiggy helped Dappled-Sun remove the lei, and Witch-Hazel tucked it safely back in her pack. No one said anything. No words seemed sufficient. They were together; they'd escaped the shadowcats again. For now. That was what mattered.

Twiggy adjusted the ropes steering the balloon, and several flaps in the rainbow fabric above them opened and closed, changing the way the wind caught, causing the whole contraption to begin sailing through the air like a runaway kite.

Fish-Breath climbed back up from the floor of the basket and watched the island dwindle into the sun-splashed distance, until the shadowcats who'd been chasing him were nothing more than invisibly small points on a tree-flecked dot.

Dappled-Sun, enamored with the mechanisms of the hot air balloon, fell easily into an animated conversation with Twiggy about the physical principles behind the balloon and how it all related to several of Occultus's projects involving tiny balloons inserted surgically into the octopus's patients.

The whole conversation made Witch-Hazel alternate between shuddering with horror and sighing with boredom.

The Otter's Wings

But mostly, she watched Fish-Breath's face as relief, terror, sadness, and ultimately a kind of lost confusion flickered over his broad, beautiful features. Anger boiled in Witch-Hazel's heart at what the Mouse King was putting them through.

With a deep breath to center herself, Witch-Hazel realized this was the time when she needed to focus on how she'd come to meet the three queens during her past journeys, and how that might help her locate the Mouse King and finally put an end to the chaos he'd been wrecking upon the world.

11

Witch-Hazel had met Amalah, salamander queen of the Fire Realm, deep in the buried and abandoned mole city, upon a pile of hoarded treasure, when she'd found and broken a bottle filled with an opalescent liquid. The broken potion had summoned Amalah to the location.

But Witch-Hazel didn't have a special potion bottle, waiting to summon a queen to her. And there were no piles of ancient treasure nearby to search for one.

She had met Mercy, the butterfly queen of the Air Realm, when she'd been asked to care for an unhatched egg, protecting it so it would have a chance to hatch.

But Witch-Hazel was unlikely to meet another monarch in that way, fetal, pre-formed, not even born.

She had met Queen Kokeu, koi queen of the Water Realm, during the horrible fight between her friends and the zombie creatures serving the snake mage when Fish-Breath had almost died. The entire battle was a chaotic blur in her memory, but she did remember a few details. The fight had been in the ruined remains of a church with beautiful stained glass windows, sadly stopped from ever shining with the glow of daylight by the dirt behind them.

The whole church had been buried, much like the mole city. And yet, it clearly hadn't been built that way originally, unlike the mole city. Because of those beautiful stained glass windows ...

As she thought about the colorful patterns on those windows and how she'd seen them shatter, she felt a twinge in her paw and looked down. There was a scar still, across the palm of her paw pads, where a broken piece of the stained glass had sliced her. She'd hoped to use it as a weapon, but instead ... The blood red glass had drawn blood from her paw, and as it dripped ... a pool had formed in the floor.

That's where Queen Kokeu had appeared. Witch-Hazel had summoned her. In fact, that's what Queen Kokeu had said to her: "You've summoned me ... with blood and desperation."

Witch-Hazel had those. She had them in abundance. Her body was boiling with blood, angry and red, and her heart was filled with desperation.

She had the ingredients to summon a queen. All she had to do was a little magic.

Before she could think about the fact that she wasn't a mage or wizard or had ever learned any magic, other than a single spell she'd read in a stolen raven's book, Witch-Hazel took her own claws from one paw to the scarred palm of the other. She sliced into the skin with her needle-sharp claw, and red blood leaked out. Wet and real. Not at all magical, just painful.

Witch-Hazel chewed her lip, thinking. What had been different when she'd summoned Queen Kokeu before? She'd used a broken shard of stained glass as her tool, instead of her own claw. But she hadn't saved it. She had nothing like that now.

What else? She'd been bearing the Celestial Fragments at that point, because it was before she'd used them to save Fish-Breath's life.

The Moon Opal was the Fragment that granted the boon of endless breath, the normal ability of a fish like Queen Kokeu. On a whim and a hope, Witch-Hazel grasped Fish-Breath's paw, pressing her flowing blood against the smooth curve of the Moon Opal encrusted in his knuckle. She felt the red liquid smear over its surface, and when she looked, she saw the sparkling colors marred—the blue, yellow, and pink flecks of brightness now dimmed by the sheen of her blood.

"You're bleeding," Fish-Breath said, confused and troubled.

"Oh, come on!" Witch-Hazel cried in frustration. She couldn't feel any of the electrifying tingle of magic flowing from the gem that she remembered from when they were flying, but then, all at once, the blood on her paw burned, sizzling, smoke rising from the opal ... no ... not smoke. Steam rolled off the Moon Opal like an early morning fog, first in tiny tendrils, and then gushing outward, filling the hot air balloon's basket. The fog rose around them like a curtain, until the basket was completely filled with the soupy fog, damp and chilly against Witch-Hazel's fur. Then it boiled over the edges of the basket like a waterfall, streaming down toward the ocean below.

"What is happening?" Twiggy asked, her teeth whistling even more than usual.

Witch-Hazel was afraid to answer, afraid to take responsibility for the magic spell she'd cast without knowing if she could, or how it would work, or whether it was safe.

Fish-Breath answered for her. "It's Moon Opal magic somehow. And blood magic, I think. I can feel the opal sizzling. It's like the blood in my paw has turned into bees. Or maybe … carbonation."

The three of them had once drunk carbonated strawberry lemonades together back in Riverton. Witch-Hazel remembered how the bubbles had stung her tongue. The fog around them started stinging her paw pads, nose, and the inside of her ears like that now. It was too thick for her to see any of her friend's faces. She couldn't tell how scared they were. And she didn't know if she'd be lying if she reassured them.

In retrospect, trying to summon a god might not be the safest magic spell for a complete beginner. Nor the best activity for inside a hot air balloon. Unfortunately, she couldn't go back and have those thoughts two minutes ago.

Witch-Hazel focused all of her mind on remembering Queen Kokeu, as if she could pull the royal koi fish directly out of her memory. She recalled the fish's red and gold scales; her fluttery fins and strangely bewhiskered face; her round mouth and rounder, coin-like eyes. But those visual details all felt hazy, like the misty world surrounding Witch-Hazel right now.

What Witch-Hazel remembered the most was the sadness in Queen Kokeu's voice, the kindness she offered during one of the worst moments of the squirrel's life. While ultimately Queen Kokeu had been unable to save all of Witch-Hazel's friends, she had tilted the balance of the battle they were fighting by spiriting away all of the undead creatures who should have crossed into her realm—the Water Realm—when they'd died.

And she'd offered to take Fish-Breath and Twiggy too. She'd offered to keep them safe.

Witch-Hazel had refused.

And Fish-Breath had nearly died.

With a held back sob, Witch-Hazel's desperation turned the corner to regret. If she had made a different choice, then her friends would already safely be in the Water Realm— "safe and happy," that's what Queen Kokeu had said, what she had offered, and what Witch-Hazel turned down.

The fog surrounding all four of the animals in the balloon turned from gray to blue in the moment when Witch-Hazel's desperation sharpened into regret. The fog thickened, changing from hazy mist into clear water, and all of a sudden, Witch-Hazel could see the others again. They were no longer in the basket of the balloon. It was gone. And so was the air. They were floating. All four of them. In a beautiful, underwater forest of kelp. And there was nothing to breathe.

Witch-Hazel's body tried to panic, but she couldn't let herself. Instead, she pulled her backpack around and dug out the air lily leis. She draped one over her own head and gasped as it settled on her shoulders, gulping up the air it provided and feeling the rising panic begin to subside. Fish-Breath grabbed the others, handed one to Twiggy, and helped wrap the third around Dappled-Sun again. The gem-encrusted otter didn't need one.

The songbird's wings were flapping erratically; she was even less of a water creature than Witch-Hazel, and yet this was her second time submerged since joining the adventurers less than an hour earlier. Witch-Hazel wondered if she already had regrets.

Witch-Hazel could see the questions plain on her friends' faces: what had happened? Where were they? How did they get here?

And Witch-Hazel wanted to answer them, but before she could open her mouth to discover if speech was even possible in this underwater world, four armored creatures—lobsters with their exo-skeletons painted in intricate patterns and gold tridents held in their impressive pincers—swam up to them. The kelp swayed in the wake of their movement.

Without words, the lobsters raised their tridents, gesturing for the travelers to swim ahead of them, into the thick veils of kelp. The sight of the lobsters' long waving antennae and shorter eyestalks reminded Witch-Hazel of her encounter long ago with the sorcerous crabs of the Order of Decapodia Crustacea. Twiggy and Fish-Breath had sworn the crabs should have been allies, devoted to protecting the endless river that had once looped from sky to land and back again. But they'd been trapped underground so long they'd gone mad, and Witch-Hazel had been forced to protect her friends with violence. At least, that's how Fish-Breath told the story.

Witch-Hazel was still haunted by the memory of the crabs' eyes slicing away under the sharp edge of her sword. She remembered the feel of it in her paws, swinging through the air, the inevitability of its damage already decided by the time she'd been struck with doubt. It had been the first truly morally questionable choice she'd made in her adventures—the crabs had attacked her with streams of water, and she'd countered their attack with cold, sharpened steel. Blinding them forever. She shuddered.

She wanted to be better than that. But it was hard to make level-headed, reasonable, morally-sound choices when her best friend was on the run from vicious shadows dead-set on clawing unearthly wounds into his body, and sometimes it seemed like she was the only thing standing between him and the end of him.

Uncertain and unprepared for facing the god she'd summoned with blood and regret, Witch-Hazel shrugged at her friends, signaling they should do as the lobsters wanted. They looked threatening, but they were probably part of Queen Kokeu's guard. And Witch-Hazel had wanted to find Queen Kokeu.

Then the squirrel led the way, paddling awkwardly with her front paws and kicking furiously with her hind paws, making slow headway swimming through the water. After a moment though, Fish-Breath rescued her—he swam up beside her, strong tail waving behind him like a paddle or a rudder or some other part of a boat. Witch-Hazel knew nothing about swimming, but she knew it got a lot easier when Fish-Breath grabbed her paw and began pulling her along.

Twiggy swam up beside them, towing Dappled-Sun. The bird had grabbed onto the shoulder strap of the beaver's sundress with her talons and folded her wings tight against her back to become more hydrodynamic.

The trident-wielding lobsters took up positions on either side of the strange band of travelers and escorted them through the kelp forest.

12

As the green ribbons of kelp thinned around her, Witch-Hazel began to make out the details of Queen Kokeu's court of the Water Realm. She had seen two courts of the elements before—Queen Amalah's fire court in a vision, dancing in the illusory flames of a dreamlike mirage. It had been a marvelous, heady place filled with tables heaped high with delicious foods and courtiers cavorting. Queen Mercy's court of air, on the other hand, had been mostly empty, as the queen had been away from her court, living among mortals for many lifetimes.

Witch-Hazel's friend Zwi, a worker bee who had ascended to become a queen bee, still lived in Queen Mercy's court, surrounded by her own worker bee daughters now. They would have filled the ivory halls and pearlescent gardens around the All-Being's castle with the smell of honey and perfume of flowers by now. Zwi would be a good courtier for any royal of the elements to have by her side.

Both the vision Witch-Hazel had seen of the fire court and what she imagined of the blossoming air court were beautiful. Hauntingly, dangerously beautiful. But Queen

Kokeu's court of water was a step beyond. It was unlike anything the squirrel had ever seen before.

Braids of kelp in brilliant shades of green—everything from pale peridot to darkly glinting emerald—were strung through the space like intricate lace. Fantastical creatures swam in every which direction, as if up and down had no meaning at all here. Except, that wasn't entirely true, because shyly dancing sunlight filtered down from above, playing across the scene like the misty golden shade of sentimentality coloring fondly remembered moments from one's youth.

And the creatures! Oh, they were completely alien. Sure, some of them were familiar—otters, beavers, lizards, frogs, and turtles—the types of animals who belonged to the Water Realm, but still primarily lived on land. But those familiar creatures wore gleaming, rainbowy bubbles around their heads, as if they were astronauts dressed in retro golden age science-fiction spacesuits—concepts Witch-Hazel knew nothing about.

Most of the creatures here were deep sea animals—beings who a squirrel would never have a chance to encounter in the course of a normal life. Witch-Hazel was not living a normal squirrel's life. She saw squid and cuttlefish with bone-pale yet fluidly boneless tentacles; fish with the strangest, brightest combinations of colors and faces like weird drawings a kit might scratch in the sand; crabs and lobsters with armored, segmented exoskeletons like terrifyingly oversized insects; and gigantic creatures with smooth, streamlined bodies, weaving their way among the kelp. Witch-Hazel had never seen dolphins or whales before, and although she'd heard they were huge, she could never have imagined the true scale of their size.

Witch-Hazel had thought the creatures in Occultus's lab were strange and alien, but they'd been made from familiar pieces. Some of the creatures here—like a fish with an appendage dangling a tiny lantern in front of its fearsome toothy maw—were unimaginably foreign and made her memory of the patchwork gryphons seem downright reasonable and normal in comparison.

Watching the scene in front of her made Witch-Hazel feel like she'd drunk too much of her sister's pear cider and the entire world had turned giggly and silly around her. If she'd been somewhere the rules of existence made any sense, Witch-Hazel would've thought she should sit down for a bit, collect her bearings. But here, she was already floating.

Through the dizzying sights around them, a pattern emerged—figures moved aside, swaying their tails or jetting their tube organs, whatever they did to swim, making space for a regal figure. Queen Kokeu cut through the water like the edge of a sword; her gold and red scales caught the lazy sunlight from above and sparkled like coins in a wishing fountain.

But Witch-Hazel knew better than to expect Queen Kokeu to grant her any wishes. She was a deity, supreme ruler of an entire elemental realm, not a mere genie in a lamp. And summoning her may have been asking for too much already.

Nonetheless, the queen's swaying route, like the bends of an ancient river, brought her through the crowds of her courtiers and the filigreed braids of kelp, directly to Witch-Hazel.

The koi fish, with her golden circlet upon her head, stared wide-eyed at the squirrel, a being entirely out of place in her court.

Queen Kokeu's mouth opened and closed in the slow way of fish, bending into a wide oval and then rounding into a perfect circle and back again. None of the four travelers intruding in her realm knew what to do or say—especially with the four trident-armed lobsters still guarding them—so they simply floated, awaiting the queen's proclamation.

Eventually, Queen Kokeu swam closer to them, close enough Witch-Hazel could see herself bizarrely reflected in those coin-like eyes. The fish lifted a translucent fin, as delicate and smooth as silk, and ran it along the air lily lei around Witch-Hazel's neck.

"Very clever," she said in a voice like a babbling brook echoing through a deep, forgotten cave. "These flowers are very rare outside my realm. You must have had help finding them." She turned her head, which meant bending her entire body, to look at Fish-Breath, sizing him up. She clearly knew where the help had come from. "I see you saved your friend after all. Perhaps at some cost to his sense of self. It's a shame I can't help him there. Those wings don't belong in my realm, but they're bound to him with a magic outside of mine. So long as he stays here, they stay too."

Queen Kokeu turned back to look at Witch-Hazel, but the squirrel found she couldn't speak. Not in this watery realm.

"Ah, you see the limits now of your clever flower ornaments." With another wave of her fin, Queen Kokeu cast glimmering bubbles around each of the visitors' heads.

The bubbles had looked strange on strangers, but they were even more bizarre adorning Witch-Hazel's friends. Twiggy looked startled by the bubble; Fish-Breath cracked a goofy, lopsided grin, as if he knew he must look even more ridiculous now—an otter with wings is one thing; an otter with wings on his back and a bubble over his head was almost too much, even for his tall tales.

Witch-Hazel couldn't read the expression on Dappled-Sun's beak though. She didn't know the songbird well enough yet.

"Try again," Queen Kokeu said. "Tell me why and how you've teleported yourself and these friends of yours into my realm, despite two of you belonging to different elements entirely and the fact that I sealed my court away from the world when I sensed my sister of the air had returned to her throne."

"Queen Mercy, you mean," Witch-Hazel said, finally finding her tongue and discovering it worked completely normally now. "My friends and I helped her return to the All-Being's castle."

"A new name," Queen Kokeu said, ponderously. "The times are truly changing. Swim with me, Witch-Hazel." The koi fish turned, bending her body like a question mark in the process.

Witch-Hazel hesitated, filled with questions and concerns—why had the queen sealed her court away? what of her friends? and how could she possibly keep up, swimming with a fish?—but Queen Kokeu would have none of it.

"Your friends will be well attended to, and you'll find you have no trouble swimming as long as you stay close by my side. My current will carry you."

So, Witch-Hazel drifted into the current beside Queen Kokeu and swam through the water court as easily as if she actually belonged there. Water slipped past her, lifting and smoothing her fur in ways the air never rustled it. Everything felt different here. Portentous. Weighty.

"Come now," Queen Kokeu said. "You've earned some lenience through your impressive display of magic,

The Otter's Wings

but do not forget: you are an intruder here. I did not invite you. And I expect answers."

"I …" Witch-Hazel faltered. She should fear this fish whose power was so much greater than hers, and yet, she didn't. She didn't know if that was folly. Or bravery. Or if there was a difference. She swallowed her feelings and said, "I remembered the last time we met, when you said I'd summoned you with blood and desperation. And so—"

"And so you cast a magical spell, spilling your own blood to pay the price and powering it with your own emotions."

"I guess I did." Witch-Hazel could still hardly believe it had worked.

"That shouldn't have been enough. It wouldn't have been, in the past."

"What do you mean?" Witch-Hazel asked. If magic was draining from the world, it seemed like casting magical spells should have become harder, not easier.

"We're in my court," Queen Kokeu said, turning sharply, swimming deeper into the kelp forest surrounding the court, buying the two of them some privacy from all the heads that turned as they swam past. "I ask the questions here. At least, for now."

"You asked 'how' and 'why,'" Witch-Hazel said, fumbling to figure out what to say. She had hoped to find help here. But she was feeling less and less sure of that hope. "I've answered 'how' as well as I can. As for 'why,' there are shadowcats chasing my friend. We've been running for days. We flew across the ocean to an island, and they still found us. I didn't know where else to turn."

"The mouse king's guard," Queen Kokeu said with a disgusted twist to her oval mouth. Her tentacle-like whiskers shivered. "It is true they cannot find you here."

Once again, the queen turned suddenly, so suddenly that Witch-Hazel splayed her paws and waved her tail trying to stop from running into her. But the koi fish had control of the currents, and the water turned the two of them until they were facing each other, floating without motion.

"I offered to take your friends into my realm before," Queen Kokeu said, "and you turned me down. I think, you wanted to stay with them."

Witch-Hazel nodded silently, not quite daring to hope for help.

"I'll make the offer again," Queen Kokeu said, "but this time I'll offer more: all four of you can stay, even the bird. I'll make you my own seneschal. You'll rule over the realm of water by my side, slightly beneath me, as befits a grand magician. Your friends will be safe and happy."

Witch-Hazel's heart leapt, but not at the offer. At the words Queen Kokeu had used to describe her—*grand magician.* She had performed one feat of magic, and she hardly knew how she'd done it. How was that enough to earn such an offer? It was too much. There had to be a reason behind it. "Why are you offering this?" Witch-Hazel asked.

"I ask the questions," Queen Kokeu repeated. In that moment, her round golden eyes reminded Witch-Hazel of the snake's eyes, the snake who had sung a song to her so long ago, lulling and luring her at the same time. "Do you accept my offer?"

For a moment, Witch-Hazel was tempted. There were other otters and beavers here. She looked back through the strands of kelp and saw her friends. They did look happy. And they were safe. She'd known, somehow even before Queen Kokeu confirmed it, that the shadowcats couldn't follow them here. The shadows were different under the sea.

But then ... She saw Dappled-Sun. The little yellow bird swam after Twiggy and Fish-Breath, wings flapping awkwardly. This wasn't what she had bargained for—well, perhaps, as a visit. But not for the rest of her life. Witch-Hazel wondered if Queen Kokeu would allow the songbird to return to the normal world, while Fish-Breath, Twiggy, and herself stayed here ...

And yet, Witch-Hazel didn't want to stay here. She had liked Riverton. She liked building her own life. She didn't want to belong to a fish queen's court any more than she'd wanted to belong to Queen Mercy's or Queen Amalah's.

"Why do all of you queens keep asking me to join your courts?" The question burst out of Witch-Hazel in frustration.

"That's a 'no'?" Queen Kokeu asked.

"That's a 'no,'" Witch-Hazel agreed.

"As I expected." The koi queen turned tail and began swimming again. The current carried Witch-Hazel along beside her. They swam together in silence for a while, and Witch-Hazel listened to the echoey sound of the crowded, colorful court around them.

When Queen Kokeu finally spoke again, her words were even more mystifying than what she'd said before: "The queens you meet keep asking you to join their courts, because we can see your crown."

"My crown?" Witch-Hazel said, at a complete loss. She had no crown. She'd once had a very fine sword, but she'd lost it long ago.

"It's like a ghostly vision above your head," Queen Kokeu said, causing the squirrel to reach up and touch the fur between her ears.

There was only fur. "I have no crown. I never have."

"You will," Queen Kokeu said. "If you have your way. It's as if you're summoning it into existence out of sheer willpower. And any royal would love to usurp your power and keep it for their own. Even me. Although, I must admit, I hoped you would answer as you have. I think

The Otter's Wings

you're the only hope to end the war that's been raging through the heavens."

"War?"

"You've seen the effects in your world. Sudden fire. Sudden rain. Queen Amalah and I have been battling, trying to claim as much of the mortal world for ourselves as we can, before everything changes."

Witch-Hazel remembered the firestorm that had led to her discovering the air lilies at the bottom of a lake, followed by the sudden rainy deluge. And she remembered many other stories, told by travelers in Riverton, of unseasonable storms, both floods and fires. It was not good for mortals when gods fought wars.

And yet, Witch-Hazel didn't want the responsibility of stopping those wars. "I don't want a crown," she said.

"Yes, you do. Everything you've done during your adventures says you do. You want the world to work a specific way, and you won't rest until it does. You'll do whatever you have to, in order to achieve your goals. And that means, one day, you will wear a crown. Or you will die trying."

Witch-Hazel didn't like those choices. And she didn't want to think about them. "I came here to help my friends. We can't escape the shadowcats."

"Let them catch you," Queen Kokeu said.

Witch-Hazel frowned. "They'll kill Fish-Breath."

"Not if you step past them. When they come to you, step onto the shadow roads they travel. Take their path to their home. Then you can face King Eiric and fight for your crown."

The koi queen's words rested as heavily on Witch-Hazel as any crown ever could.

"For now, you and your friends are welcome to stay here as long as you like. Rest. Enjoy yourselves. And when you're ready to leave, simply swim towards the sky." Queen Kokeu's fins fluttered at her sides, and her mouth thinned from a circle into a tightly stretched oval. "But remember, I made my offer, and you refused it. I will not make it again. Mortal lives are short, and you can stay here for the rest of yours if you'd like anyway. I'll hardly notice. But do not ask me to reiterate my offer. You had your chance, and you made your choice."

Queen Kokeu swam away before Witch-Hazel could object to the idea that she might change her mind. She swam like sunlight gleaming on a pond; here one moment, bright and overwhelming, and far away the next. The squirrel no longer found herself swept along in the koi's current.

13

Witch-Hazel dogpaddled awkwardly through the royal court, only saved from bumping into every creature between herself and her friends by the fact that everyone else here swam better than she did. Scales, fur, fins, paws ... It didn't matter. Every one of them was at home in the Water Realm, except for her. And once she arrived at where her friends were floating, Dappled-Sun too, of course. The songbird had settled for clinging with her talons to the strap of Twiggy's sundress again. The ruffles of the dress flowed especially prettily in this underwater world. And as Witch-Hazel watched Twiggy's face, she saw more happiness there than she'd seen in a long time.

Then Fish-Breath turned toward her, and his wide grin could've knocked her breathless, no matter how many air lily leis she wore or bubbles surrounded her head. She could tell from his face, immediately, that he'd been telling tall tales and jokes, and that here, people were responding to them the way he expected. The way he remembered, from before he'd become a strange, mythical, tall tale of a creature himself.

Because in the court of a god, a winged otter doesn't necessarily stand out.

Fish-Breath reached a webbed paw out and grasped Witch-Hazel's paw. "Have you tried the candied clams?" he asked.

"What?" Witch-Hazel asked, still lost in her own reveries, more than half of her mind devoted to Queen Kokeu's final words to her.

"Here, let me show you," Fish-Breath said. He waved his thick tail, propelling them both through the water toward an eddy the size of a small shrub. He reached his free paw in and grabbed a fistful of glittery pink objects, like small pebbles. He pulled them out of the tiny whirlpool and offered them to Witch-Hazel.

Gingerly, Witch-Hazel tried one. It was indeed a sugar-encrusted clam—chewy, sweet, fishy, and weirdly delicious. She stared at the swirling water, filled with the candied clams, keeping them localized in one spot instead of floating all over the place, and she had no idea how it worked. Why did it stay in one place? She reached a paw toward it herself, and as the water flowed around her knuckles, ruffling her fur, she felt the warm tingle she'd come to think of the sign of magic.

She pulled her paw back quickly, as if the tiny tornado had burned her. Looking around the court, she saw many more of them.

"Isn't it wonderful here?" Fish-Breath asked.

It was.

They could stay forever.

And Fish-Breath and Twiggy would be happy.

And safe.

And it made Witch-Hazel feel like she was dying inside. She didn't belong here. And she didn't want to belong here. She supposed that was how Fish-Breath and Twiggy had felt about living in Riverton, misunderstood, mocked, and cast aside by people they'd known since they were young. And Witch-Hazel felt bad about trying to make them stay there. But living out their days in the hazy blur of revelry in Queen Kokeu's water court wasn't the answer. There had to be a better place. A better way. Somewhere—some way—all of them could be happy.

Ruefully, Witch-Hazel realized this had to be what Queen Kokeu meant about her summoning a crown for herself into existence through sheer willpower. She wouldn't settle for a world that wasn't good enough. Not when there was anything she could do to make it better.

"We have to go," Witch-Hazel tried to tell Fish-Breath, but the otter had already begun swimming away, drawn by the allure of another eddy, filled with some other kind of spinning whirl of tasty treats. Frustrated, Witch-Hazel tried to swim after him, and when her paws floundered uselessly through the water, she found herself wondering about the currents that had allowed her to follow Queen Kokeu so easily.

The koi queen wasn't large enough for wakes to truly form in the water beside her when she swam. They must have been magical. Like the twirling eddies of treats.

Witch-Hazel stopped trying to swim and simply twirled a paw in the water, focusing on the tingly feel she remembered every time she touched the Celestial Fragments. She felt the water whirling with her paw, but it seemed no different than the normal sensation she'd get from the movement of the water.

But when her paw stopped moving, the water kept twirling. Not for very long. But longer than it should have.

Witch-Hazel opened her paws wide and faced them, palm forward, toward Fish-Breath. She reached with everything in her mind and body and essence, trying to draw herself toward the winged otter.

And it was hard to be sure, but she thought, maybe, the way she was floating in the water, bobbing with the random currents caused by so many courtiers swimming past, changed. She thought, *maybe,* she was floating toward Fish-Breath more than she should have been.

Witch-Hazel closed her paws and stopped trying to move herself like some arcane wizard from a fairy story. She had seen so much magic in the world, and yet, it was still hard for her to believe that somehow, she'd gained the ability to channel that magic.

It didn't fit with the story she'd been told. And yet, she could feel it flowing through her paws, warm and effervescent. She'd been feeling it whenever she touched Fish-Breath's encrusted gems for some time, and now, she could make it happen with the power of sheer determination.

If magic was draining out of the world, then why could a perfectly normal—albeit stubborn—squirrel like her suddenly perform magical feats unseen by any mortal animals she knew within many lifetimes?

Suddenly, Witch-Hazel was startled by a cheerful otter face, upside down, right in front of her own, so close the magical bubbles over their heads were almost touching. It was Fish-Breath, grinning widely. In her reverie, she'd lost track of him in the crowd and hadn't noticed.

"Hah!" Fish-Breath exclaimed. "You didn't see me coming!" Then swam away, as if they were both kits playing a game of tag.

Witch-Hazel smiled, perhaps a little sadly, at his happiness and tilted her own head, even though he'd already swum away, as if she were trying to straighten out the sight of him. Flip him back the right way up.

The motion of tilting her head, changing the angle of the world around her, was such a small thing; it shouldn't have mattered. But sometimes, the biggest realizations come to us suddenly, out of the blue, or maybe the chaos, and they crystallize into a thought. An entirely new thought. Something that feels so obvious, you can hardly believe you hadn't thought of it before.

And that's when Witch-Hazel knew: magic wasn't draining out of the world. The cracks in the Sun, Moon, and North Star might have released pent up stores of magic, but it wasn't flowing *out* of the world. That story was upside down.

The magic was flowing *in*.

For countless mortal lifetimes, magic had been the providence of the All-Being and the royal heads of the four elemental realms. But now, it was washing through the world, ungoverned, unmitigated, uncontrolled. Free. Available to a squirrel like her.

The loss of control over magic—being no longer able to keep it for themselves—must have felt to the All-Being and queens like the magic was draining away entirely. But it wasn't. It was merely draining away from them. Away from the immortal beings who had told her the story of what was happening.

But this was a story she needed to figure out for herself. A story she would be required to write the end of, and she needed to be sure of what had happened—what was still happening—in order to be certain of her choices.

But if she was right, then what the mouse king had done in rending cracks into those three celestial bodies may have been a boon to the world, not the sign of a catastrophic ending.

Perhaps, in spite of the shadowcats, he was on their side. Maybe the shadowcats were only a misunderstanding.

She needed to find him.

But then she saw Fish-Breath and Twiggy dancing together in the distance, caught up in a whirling line of dancers, tracing their away across the court, shaking their tails and fins and tentacles to the tempo of a tinkling melody that floated through the water like a brightly colored line of threads in a tapestry, binding everything together, making everything ebb and flow with a breath-like rhythm. Even Dappled-Sun looked happy, flapping her wings to the beat, perched on Twiggy's shoulder.

Fish-Breath and Twiggy had traveled so far with Witch-Hazel, facing so much fear and strain. So much potential loss. With so few breaks to rest. She couldn't rip her friends from this place of solace. Not right away.

And so she swam forward, easing the awkwardness of her paws in the water with the grace she could imagine in her mind, granting it to her paws through the power of the tingly magic flowing through the world. It was becoming easier and easier for her to control it. In a deep part of her mind, that worried her. She was changing. And the implications of those changes had the potential to be very far-reaching. But she didn't want to think about that yet.

So she swam to Fish-Breath, returned the smile he gave her, and took ahold of his paw. Twiggy grabbed her other paw. And together they danced. They feasted. Then they danced some more. And when they tired themselves out, they slept in braided hammocks of emerald green kelp. Twiggy and Dappled-Sun shared one hammock; Witch-Hazel and Fish-Breath shared another. Curled against her beloved otter's chest, Witch-Hazel watched the unending revelries until the swaying of the hammock in the ocean currents, the steady, drowsy rhythm of Fish-Breath's breathing, and the gentle sound of the music lulled her to sleep.

14

When Witch-Hazel awoke—from deep dreams that immediately dissipated and yet made more sense in their mundanity than the fantastical quality of the real world around her—she felt more deeply rested than she'd felt in years.

Fish-Breath's breathing had changed; he was awake too, and he squeezed her, showing he'd noticed she'd joined him in consciousness. Whatever had caused Witch-Hazel to awaken so suddenly seemed to have affected Twiggy as well—the beaver was blearily rubbing her eyes, still struggling with the transition between being asleep and awake. Dappled-Sun, however, was perched high on one end of the hammock, looking wide awake and standing tall. She could've been a rooster, awake with the dawn, and ready to draw everyone else into wakefulness with her.

And yet, it wasn't dawn. Or midday. Or even night. The sunlight still filtered down from above in its lazy golden glow. Nothing had changed. The revelry continued, exactly as it had before.

Then Fish-Breath said something that felt fateful and deeply unfair: "I wish we could stay here forever."

Witch-Hazel had known he was happy here. She hadn't realized he loved it in the Water Realm quite that much. Though, she supposed, she shouldn't be surprised. He was a jovial creature of water—not only was this his realm, it was an endless party.

She didn't want to stay. But he did. And if he knew he could … he might not leave with her. She would have to choose between him and the world.

But he didn't know.

And Witch-Hazel didn't have to tell him.

No, no, that wasn't fair.

Witch-Hazel had lied to her friends before, and she'd regretted it, back in the dark tunnels deep underground. As much as she wanted to leave this place, she didn't want to be that person—someone who lied to her friends, keeping secrets for her own benefit, as if she were the only person in the world who needed to know anything, as if she were the only person who should get to make informed choices.

She didn't want lies between her and Fish-Breath. Or Twiggy. So, Witch-Hazel said what she felt she had to: she told the truth. The whole truth. "Actually, we can stay." The words felt like ash on her tongue, and she couldn't look at Fish-Breath as she said them, so she simply stared out at the chaotic revelry. "The queen invited us to stay forever."

The Otter's Wings

When Witch-Hazel brought herself to twist around and look at Fish-Breath, who was still curled up in the hammock with her, she saw surprise more than delight filling his round, bewhiskered face. He hadn't expected Witch-Hazel to have the power to grant his wish. He hadn't expected it to be granted at all.

Sometimes a wish makes more sense when it's clearly impossible. When it becomes practical, a wish is nothing more than a different choice, an option available to you, no longer a distant, desperately clung-to desire.

A fish flitting through a pond is a bright spot of gold, full of possibility, like a coin in a wishing well. But a fish in the paw ... it's cold and wriggly and squirming and alive. You can eat it. Or let it go. Either way, it's just a fish. Not a dream.

Dappled-Sun was the first to speak, she twittered in her beautiful voice, "I don't want to stay. I'm glad I came, but I didn't leave on an adventure yesterday to find myself settled down at the bottom of the ocean today. I'd like to go home. Or ... better yet ... keep adventuring."

At least, whatever else happened, Witch-Hazel wouldn't leave the Water Realm alone. And at some level, she thanked the stars for Dappled-Sun's presence and desire to leave, because it obligated her to see the songbird safely away. If it weren't for that, she knew, deep in the corners of her heart, there was a chance she'd let Fish-Breath talk her into staying here forever. She truly didn't know if she could turn him down, not if he decided to stay and asked her to stay with him.

But she hoped he wouldn't stay.

"I have to leave too," Witch-Hazel said. "I think the queens and the All-Being have been lying to us. I don't think magic is draining out of the world. I think ... it's draining in."

"What does that mean?" Dappled-Sun asked, tilting her yellow head inquisitively.

Witch-Hazel looked at both Fish-Breath's face and Twiggy's, seeking some sign of engagement or curiosity, but both the otter and the beaver seemed lost in deep contemplation. They had been offered something precious, something almost too precious to contemplate, and then, without so many words, they'd been asked to turn it down. Because now, they were looking at a choice between departing this magic realm ... and parting ways with a friend.

They needed time to think. Witch-Hazel tried to grant it to them, tried to look away from the deeply personal expressions flitting across their faces, and focus instead on explaining everything to Dappled-Sun—the details of her long journey, all the things she'd learned during her travels, and the meaning of her latest speculation.

Dappled-Sun listened intently, and when Witch-Hazel had finished speaking, there was a moment of awkward silence between them. The squirrel felt vulnerable and uncertain, painfully aware of the giant leaps she'd taken in reaching her final conclusion. She had felt so sure of it inside her own mind, but spoken out loud in clumsy words, it became something others could judge. And disagree with. No matter how certain Witch-Hazel felt of herself, she still doubted she could defend her beliefs. And she doubted anyone else would see that she was right.

Finally, Dappled-Sun spoke: "I've watched Occultus's studies for years now—helping her write up the data and results from her experiments. And I think you're right."

"What do you mean?" Witch-Hazel asked, puzzled about what Occultus's scientific studies had to do with the ebb and flow of magic.

"The bizarre things Occultus does in her lab …" Dappled-Sun flapped her wings restively. "They didn't used to work. She assumed … her skills were improving, and that's why her grand experiments work now. But …" The bird shook her head. "They should never work. The gryphons she makes? They were dead creatures. She's not giving them life with the science she believes in. It's magic. Even if Occultus doesn't think so. I've been sure of it for some time, and now, I understand how."

"Because magic is increasing in the world," Witch-Hazel said.

"Yes," Dappled-Sun agreed. "It's the best explanation. Although, I don't think it's quite that simple. Because the gryphons—the original gryphons, the natural ones—were magical, and they've all but died out. All except Mother. So, it's less like magic is increasing and more like …" She faltered for the right word.

Witch-Hazel provided it: " …it's equalizing."

Fish-Breath still looked lost in thought, but Twiggy had started paying attention to the conversation between squirrel and songbird. The beaver's pinched face, elongated by the two front teeth, looked longer and more pensive than usual. "You think the advancements of science … advancements that have happened in our lifetime or the ones just before us … have hinged on the flow of magic?"

Witch-Hazel blinked. She hadn't meant to shake Twiggy's entire worldview, but … "Yes, it seems that way."

"My hot air balloon, the electric lights in Riverton …" Twiggy trailed off, but Witch-Hazel could see in her face that she was taking account of every piece of technology, every scientific advancement she'd ever enjoyed, learned about, or invented herself. "It's all because the endless rivers between the earth and the sky dried up. Everything I've devoted my life to … would have been impossible if the magic that kept those rivers flowing had … stayed in the rivers."

Now Fish-Breath snapped back to attention. He looked squarely at Twiggy, not either of the others, as he asked: "You really think so?"

Witch-Hazel felt slighted. He didn't want to know what she thought. Or rather, he already knew, and he didn't trust it. He didn't believe her enough to just accept her description of the situation and move on from there. He needed to know what Twiggy believed before he could form his own opinion.

Witch-Hazel had thought she was past feeling jealous of their friendship. But then, she hadn't expected to find herself in their version of heaven, asking them to leave with her. Reject heaven.

"I think …" Twiggy's words were slow in coming, ponderous, each one thought out carefully. "I think it makes sense out of a lot of things. Science and magic are two sides of the same coin. I've always known that, but …"

"But there's a difference between knowing it abstractly and actually watching the coin flip over," Witch-Hazel said.

"I need more time," Fish-Breath said, turning his attention to Witch-Hazel. "Don't make me decide right now."

Time didn't seem to mean anything in Queen Kokeu's realm. It flowed as freely as water. Witch-Hazel was afraid if she gave her friends time to make their choice, decades would pass like minutes in this strange realm.

But what difference would it make? Everyone she cared about was here. She'd said goodbye to her family, as far as she was concerned, when they left Daffodil's nest.

She'd never intended to go back. Her friend Zwi, the honeybee queen, already lived in her own magical realm in the gardens outside the All-Being's castle. Time would pass as strangely there as here.

Why not wait here forever?

"As much time as you need," she said. Then looking at Dappled-Sun, she asked, "Is that okay? You wanted to go on adventures. Were you planning to go back home? Do you have family and friends you were hoping to return to?"

Dappled-Sun flapped her wings in an abjuring shrug. "I wanted to travel. I'm not worried about returning home." She would follow Witch-Hazel's lead.

And so, Fish-Breath and Twiggy returned to the dancing, feasting, and general merriment in the everlasting party under the ocean. Dappled-Sun rode along, clinging to Twiggy's shoulder strap for a while, but eventually she returned to the hammocks, where Witch-Hazel had stayed.

The squirrel wasn't interested in partying. She was interested in understanding her growing connection to the magic that flowed and sloshed through the world like floodwater after a big storm in a town not built to handle rain, gushing over sidewalks, pooling in the middle of the street, and generally causing chaos.

The Otter's Wings

Dappled-Sun brought snacks to Witch-Hazel, and the squirrel juggled them in the currents, practicing moving them through the water with the power of her mind.

"I don't understand why I can do this," Witch-Hazel said. "All of sudden, Queen Kokeu calls me a grand magician, and I can do magic unlike anything I've ever done before. It's like she made me into a magician by calling me one."

"You're sure you couldn't do tricks like this before?"

Witch-Hazel stared levelly at the songbird perched in the neighboring hammock. "I think I would have noticed."

"Maybe it's the place, then," Dappled-Sun suggested.

Witch-Hazel narrowed her eyes and held out a paw. She felt the currents of magic and water flow past her, caressing the bare skin of her paw pads and ruffling her silver fur. "Yes, maybe," she agreed. "I guess it would make sense that, even if magic in the world is equalizing, there's still more of it in Queen Kokeu's realm than, say, a random city by a river, built by beavers and otters."

"Perhaps that's why Occultus had so much luck with her experiments," Dappled-Sun theorized. "Gryffindell Isle had more magic in it, from being the home of the gryphons, than other places. And as the magic flowed out of the gryphon family line …"

"It flowed into Occultus's experiments, yes." The more they talked about it, and the more she focused on feeling the magic around her, the more certain Witch-Hazel felt of their conclusions.

The mouse king—Eiric, according to Queen Kokeu—had fundamentally changed the nature of their world by cracking open the Sun, Moon, and North Star. And healing those cracks couldn't possibly undo all of the damage that had been done.

But was it damage? Or was the world ... better this way?

Twiggy's inventions were wonderful. Occultus's experiments were terrifying. But then, natural magic seemed to oscillate equally wildly between miraculous and horrifying. This new egalitarian form of magic was no worse. And quite honestly, it was what Witch-Hazel was used to. These changes in the world had begun long before she was born, generations ago. A world where magic had been decentralized was the only kind of world she'd ever known. Everything else was mere stories.

Perhaps when she found King Eiric, and he withdrew the unwarranted pursuit of his shadowcat minions, she would thank him for changing the world.

Though she would have a hard time feeling thankful—for anything—if Fish-Breath stayed here.

Sunlight danced, music played, the festivities continued, and time passed. Witch-Hazel didn't know how much. She imagined leaving without her friends; she imagined having never come to Queen Kokeu's realm in the first place. And the difference between her imagined scenarios and reality grew blurry, like the hazy view of a mirage.

But finally, Fish-Breath and Twiggy returned to the hammocks among the kelp, looking somber, and ready to state their choice.

15

Witch-Hazel's heart grew cold. She wished she'd left already. She didn't want to hear Fish-Breath choose against her. She'd rather have made the choice herself.

But then the otter said, "We're ready."

"Ready?" Witch-Hazel asked uncertainly, voice quavering.

"To leave," Twiggy said.

A sob caught in Witch-Hazel's throat, but she held her voice steady as she said, "I didn't think you'd come."

"I have more inventions to make and discoveries to uncover," Twiggy said. "I'm not done with the real world yet."

"This isn't life," Fish-Breath added. "It's an afterlife. And I'm not ready for that. Especially not with these cumbersome wings still on my back, throwing off my balance and tweaking all my other muscles." He flapped the wings slowly through the water around them, wincing as they moved. The feathered limbs certainly didn't look as hydrodynamic as they were aerodynamic.

Witch-Hazel understood better why Fish-Breath disliked the wings so much now that she was down here, surrounded by water. She would never move smoothly through water. But he used to. And now, he had to clamp the wings uselessly against his back to recapture that fluid movement.

Witch-Hazel wondered if she'd been in an afterlife suited perfectly to her own desires and proclivities—as this place seemed to be for Fish-Breath's, even if it did come with a slight catch in that he'd have to keep his wings—if she'd have the same strength to give it up. The fortitude to cast aside paradise and continue with her real life ... That was impressive. But then, looking at Twiggy and Fish-Breath's faces, she realized, it wouldn't matter how perfect of a realm she discovered. If it didn't have her friends, it wouldn't be able to hold her.

Maybe giving up paradise isn't so hard, because maybe, there's not really any such thing. It's all just life.

"So, how do we get to this mad mouse king?" Twiggy asked.

"We swim up," Witch-Hazel said. "And when we get back to the normal world, we wait for the shadowcats to come. When they do ..." She shivered, in spite of the perfect temperature of the water where they were floating. "We take their shadow roads to the Earthen Realm."

For a moment, watching her friends faces, Witch-Hazel was sure Fish-Breath and Twiggy were about to change their minds. But then the otter nodded, resolute, and the beaver turned her eyes upwards. "Just swim?" she asked.

"That's what Queen Kokeu said," Witch-Hazel agreed.

Fish-Breath grabbed her paw, and Twiggy held out an arm toward Dappled-Sun. The songbird hopped from hammock to wrist then shuffled up to the beaver's shoulder. Then the two strong swimmers of the group—beaver and otter—flipped their tails and kicked their paws, propelling the whole group upward.

They swam through the emerald green kelp. They swam past the dancing revelers. They swam and swam, Witch-Hazel helping to push them along by smoothing the currents around them, manipulating the flow of magic until it caused the water to practically pull them upward.

As they swam, the music grew quieter, falling into the distance. The water grew colder. And Witch-Hazel felt her hold on the magic growing thinner. But she squeezed Fish-Breath's paw, and more magic flowed into her body, warm and tingly. She felt the smoothness of the Moon Opal on his knuckle, and she pulled magic through it like it was a conduit.

When they passed through the ethereal transition from Queen Kokeu's realm into the open ocean of the real world, Witch-Hazel sensed the bubble around her head trying to pop, unsupported by the queen's magic any longer. But she reinforced it—and the bubbles around her friends' heads as well—with her own magic, drawn through the Moon Opal.

All four of them continued to breathe safely, protected by her magic, until they emerged, breaking the surface of the wild ocean. Then the bubbles popped, and the salt air rushed in. Sea spray stung Witch-Hazel's eyes, and the water felt unbearably cold. There was no land in sight. Only the grayness of the ocean under the grayness of the sky, stretched in every direction, bucking and breaking, wild and inhospitable.

For a shivering moment, Witch-Hazel regretted her choice to leave the warmth and merriment of Queen Kokeu's realm. Then she saw a sliver of land in the distance. She pointed with her free paw and yelled over the roar of the waves and wind, "That way!"

The otter and beaver swam, pulling the squirrel and songbird with them. The waves grew harsher as they approached the sliver of beach, thrashing and roaring, until the water threw them all ashore, ejecting them unceremoniously from the ocean.

The sand was rough against Witch-Hazel's cheek, as she lay tumbled in the tumultuous surf, exhausted from her efforts, both magical and physical. Fish-Breath stood up and shook out his wings, flapping them until the water flew from them, making tiny rainbows in the gray light. Witch-Hazel couldn't tell the time of day; the clouds were too thick above them.

The Otter's Wings

"Is this Gryffindell Isle?" Twiggy asked.

"No, I don't think so," Dappled-Sun answered. "I've never seen a beach like this one on any of the islands around Gryffindell."

Witch-Hazel pushed herself up, raising her head above the rise and fall of the surf, and saw a look of sadness on the beaver's face that she would have bet anything was entirely for the loss of her hot air balloon.

But they didn't need a balloon for the next leg of their travels. Only shadows.

In the gray light of the overcast day, shadows were nowhere and everywhere. But then Witch-Hazel looked inland and saw trees. She dragged herself up to her feet and began trudging across the sand, making a point to catch Fish-Breath's paw again as she passed him. Her waterlogged tail felt too heavy to fly like the proud flag it should be; instead, she let it drag across the wet sand, leaving a strange trail.

When they came to the trees, Witch-Hazel settled down to wait. The shadowcats would come.

Fish-Breath settled beside her. Twiggy, however, busied herself, gathering driftwood and broken twigs from the base of the trees. Dappled-Sun flew beside her, carrying some of the smaller twigs in her talons, seemingly curious as to the beaver's intentions for all the building supplies. The bird had found herself a new scientist to assist.

Witch-Hazel watched the twigs and driftwood turn into a small shelter around them, feeling guilty for not helping. Even Fish-Breath had begun helping Twiggy arrange the supplies to match the pattern in her mind, but Witch-Hazel couldn't risk the distraction of letting her paws get caught up in the work of manual labor. She had to focus on the shadows. She had to be ready for the shadowcats when they came.

When they found Fish-Breath, she would have only moments to figure out how to step past them onto a pathway that sounded like a story kits might make up for a pretend game.

Her whole life had become a game of pretend.

When the shadows stretched across the shore, signaling the fall of night, Witch-Hazel worried the shadowcats might never find them here. She'd sensed no sign of them. She was half inclined to believe everything fantastical she'd ever encountered—every shred of magic that had passed through her paws and every mythical being she'd met—was nothing more than the mad ravings, the desperate hallucinations of a lost squirrel, stranded on an island, cut off from the rest of the world.

What made more sense—she had met ghost moles, a necromancer snake, the last gryphon and last unicorn, and been asked to join the courts of three queens, not to mention visiting the All-Being's castle in the sky—or her friends had tried to fly across the ocean in a hot air balloon, crashed within range of this island, and she'd imagined it all?

Wouldn't it be simple and peaceful to just be lost, instead of to feel the weight of the world and magic's role in it pressing down on her shoulders?

But whether or not it would be simpler, more believable, or even what she'd prefer, Witch-Hazel was not lost and hallucinating. She was coldly, calmly aware of her surroundings, and keenly focused on the quality of the shadows as night fell on their island.

Twiggy built a campfire on the edge of the sand, and Fish-Breath swam in the surf until he'd caught an abundance of fish for them to roast. Different fish than he'd used to catch in the river by Riverton. These were ocean fish, and their taste was salty and exotic. As the moon rose and stars began to fill the dark sky, Twiggy continued fiddling with the driftwood she'd gathered, but Fish-Breath settled into telling stories to Dappled-Sun. The songbird was a new audience, and he relished the opportunity to tell the entire story—rich with every possible detail—of his adventures with Twiggy and Witch-Hazel to someone who actually believed him.

And why wouldn't she? None of his stories were more unbelievable than the endless party Dappled-Sun had observed first-hand in the Water Realm.

The others relaxed in the soft moonlight, but Witch-Hazel's body was tense from her flexed claws to the tufted tips of her twitching ears. Her tail, finally dry again, jerked about like a flag on a windy day. Every fiber of her body was tuned into the feel of the shadows around them—she'd never noticed before tonight the different flavor of moon shadows—softer and sweeter as they fell on her fur—than those cast by sunlight. Nor the smoky, erratic flavor of shadows cast by a crackling fire. Until now, a shadow had been a shadow. But now, some of them carried danger, and she had to be ready.

When the danger found them, Witch-Hazel's newly discovered magical abilities would be the only thing standing between Fish-Breath and further mortal wounds caused by shadowy paws and claws. And her powers were completely untested. Witch-Hazel had to be ready to perform a feat she'd never performed before; she had to be ready to protect Fish-Breath from creatures who'd wounded him terribly the last time they'd caught up with him.

The poor squirrel was a wreck of nerves by the time she felt the flavor of the shadows change to something entirely new and foreign. She'd never thought about the taste of shadows before tonight, and yet, she'd lived in a world filled with them. She knew shadows. Every squirrel who lived had to know shadows—it was how they hid from hungry hawks and fearsome falcons, blending their gray fur into the gray shade cast by branches and leaves.

And this shadow didn't belong.

It felt like it had been cast by a faraway star. It was a shadow that belonged on an entirely different world.

"Fish-Breath, come here!" Witch-Hazel called, trying to contain her panic, and thinking only of protecting him. She reached her paws toward where he lounged on the other side of the fire. Hearing the timbre of her voice, the otter didn't hesitate to leap to his feet, step nimbly around the fire, and grab ahold of her paws.

"What is it?" Fish-Breath asked.

Witch-Hazel's voice fell into a husky whisper, wracked by fear: "They're coming."

Fish-Breath squeezed her paws reassuringly, and then let go of her with one paw and held it out toward Twiggy. The beaver took his paw, and with her free one, she held up a wrist for Dappled-Sun to perch on. Thus, the adventurers were all connected when the shivery feeling of a doorway opening, letting in a draft from another place, fell over Witch-Hazel. All of a sudden, her fear melted away, because she knew what to do. The danger was here, and just like Queen Kokeu had said, all she had to do was step past it—step past the shadowcats and go through the door into the shadows they'd opened.

It was like turning her head ever so slightly, changing the angle, so she could see past an obstacle in her view. Or maybe, it was simply like realizing something—a small detail that changed everything about a story, and suddenly, her perspective was different. She couldn't have described it with her fumbling tongue. She'd never been much of a storyteller. But later, Fish-Breath would say it was like Witch-Hazel had tugged on his paw, and all the shadows had changed direction. He would one day compare the experience to a solar eclipse—the moment of totality when the moon blocks the sun and all the warmth falls away from the world, and it feels as if you can finally understand the distance between solar bodies that are impossibly far apart.

But the adventurers hadn't lived through a solar eclipse yet, and so at that time, none of them had the words. All they had were sensations, jumbled and confusing, as they tumbled through the shadow roads and emerged under an entirely foreign light, shining and reflecting, refracting all around them, in the very depths of King Eiric's Earthen Realm.

16

Witch-Hazel had expected the shadowcats' path through the world's shadows to lead to a place of darkness. Startled by the intense, bright light, she turned her face down, squinting and trying to protect her eyes. Fish-Breath still held one of her paws, but she held the free one up, shielding her vision.

They were surrounded by crystals. Every color of the rainbow glittered in smooth facets, curving around them and over them like a gigantic geode. And in the center, a sphere of light swirled and shone, hanging above them like a star captured and drawn down from the heavens. It was as large as the crown of an ancient oak tree, brighter than the light of the full moon, and calling to her with its magic.

Witch-Hazel tasted the flavor of moonlight, sunlight, and starlight, all mixed together, shining outward from the strange sphere. For a moment, she thought the passageway through the shadows had thrown her and her friends into the heavens somehow, but then she moved her right hind paw, scratching her claws against the dirt under her feet. It was real and earthy. She crouched down, getting her whiskers close to the ground, and she felt the muffled echoes of thick earth stretching out around them. Wherever they were, it wasn't the heavens. She was farther underground than she'd ever been before, even when she'd been trapped in the labyrinth, led there by a singing snake. She could tell by the vibrations in the Earth, reverberating in her whiskers. Except, she shouldn't have been able to tell something like that. It had to be magic. More magic that she'd expected to find down here.

A figure approached them, walking toward the group from beneath the glowing sphere, casting a long shadow forward. The figure was silhouetted by the light, making it impossible to make out its exact features.

Nervously, Witch-Hazel turned, looking all around them, realizing she needed to understand the lay of the land here if she was going to defend her friends.

The crystalline dome, glittering with blinding light, extended all around them, with wooden structures—ladders, platforms, and trellises built along its concave surface, reaching up and around the glowing ball of light. Behind them, not far enough away for comfort, Witch-Hazel saw the shadowcats lurking, five of them in a row. Their features were no easier to make out than those of the figure approaching from the other direction, even though the glowing sphere's light shone directly upon them, but their feline shapes were unmistakable. They stood ominously between her group and a dark passageway out of the gigantic geode. It was the only exit she saw anywhere.

Once again, Witch-Hazel found herself wishing for swords in her paws. She'd never thought of herself as a violent type of squirrel ... but she sure did miss her old swords a lot.

On the other paw ... now she could do magic.

Witch-Hazel squeezed Fish-Breath's paw, the one with the Moon Opal, and she felt the glowing sphere calling to the gem encrusting his knuckle. They were connected.

"I've been waiting for you," the silhouetted figure said. It stepped closer, and the reflected light from the crystals all around illuminated the shape of a mouse, wearing regal robes and a simple golden crown between his round ears. He held his long tail in his paws. "You've done an impressive job of eluding my feline followers. But now it's time to hand over the gemstones you've stolen."

Twiggy blinked, and Fish-Breath guffawed.

"Stolen?!?" Witch-Hazel exclaimed, outraged. "I found those gemstones, lost and discarded! In fact, come to think of it, one of them was even a gift from Queen Amalah of the Fire Realm!"

"It wasn't hers to give," the mouse king quipped. He held out a paw, stepping closer. In spite of the long, intimidating shadow, he was very small. Barely half Witch-Hazel's height, making him knee-high to Fish-Breath and Twiggy. Even smaller than Dappled-Sun.

"The way I've heard the story," Witch-Hazel countered, "you stole the Celestial Fragments from the sky in the first place, breaking open the Sun, the Moon, and the North Star."

The mouse king stamped his tiny foot and wrung his long tail between his paws. "They all have Celestial Bodies to hold their magic! The Sun for Amalah's Fire Realm, the Moon for Queen Kokeu of the Water, and the North Star for that flighty butterfly queen of the Air Realm. But where is the Celestial Body of the Earthen Realm?" he asked, archly, his voice barely avoiding turning into a furious squeak. "Where is my magic? Am I not as worthy of magic as they are?! Where is my celestial body???"

The petulant look on the mouse king's face stretched into a wide, eerie grin, and he gestured above himself at the swirling ball of light. The shadow cast by his arm stretched all the way to Fish-Breath's webbed hind paws. "Well, I made myself one. I made my own star."

With a sinking feeling, Witch-Hazel realized King Eiric had never intended for magic to flow freely through the world, not any more than the three queens who had invited her to join their courts. He'd been trying to bottle it up for himself, locked inside a new celestial body. The magic she'd felt with her own paws, flowing through the world, was an unintended side-effect—a mere leak as the magic flowed through the Celestial Fragments into this artificial star, a reservoir designed to hold magic. Probably

The Otter's Wings

a leak King Eiric would like to put an end to, pulling all the left-over magic into his own, personal celestial body.

This mad mouse king was not on her side. Or anyone's but his own. He was not a good king. And she didn't, for a second, trust him to care about Fish-Breath's well-being when he took the Celestial Fragments from the otter's body. The damage caused by the shadowcat's claws had never been a mistake.

And yet, Witch-Hazel had to try for a peaceful solution, so she asked, softly, "If you have a whole star of your own, why do you need the broken-off pieces we have?"

"My star is unstable," the mouse king answered simply. "I didn't realize until too late that I would need the original broken fragments from the other celestial bodies to tie their magic together into my new star. By the time the star's instability was clear ..." He frowned. "My Celestial Fragments had been lost for lifetimes. And then, on top of that, they were stolen." His eyes narrowed, and he whipped the tip of his tail against one of his tiny palms, as if he were imagining meting out punishment to those who had stolen the Celestial Fragments.

Witch-Hazel and her friends would find no allies here. They would have been safer hiding in Queen Kokeu's realm forever. Now they were facing a mad king, surrounded by his shadowcats. And other shadowy figures lurked on the wooden walkways built around the trapped star. Surely, they were King Eiric's minions as well and would also fight for him.

Witch-Hazel had led her friends into the metaphorical lion's den. Except the lion was a mouse, and the fate of magic in the whole world might depend on whether the lion ate them.

For a moment, Witch-Hazel was overwhelmed with exhaustion, and all she wanted to do was beg King Eiric to remove the Celestial Fragments from Fish-Breath carefully and let them all leave. They could go back to Riverton. Everything could go back to the way she'd wanted it to be, before she'd discovered the power magic gave her. And the delights magic brought to the world.

She looked up at the swirling light of the star, and gazed around the geode-like cavern, seeing the sparkling colors in all the faceted crystals. It made her think of the rainbow pattern on Twiggy's hot air balloon. Would Twiggy's inventions still work if King Eiric bound the Celestial Fragments up into his artificial star? Would there be enough magic left, sloshing around the world, to power all of Riverton's gadgets? Would they still have electric light to keep the tavern warm and cozy until late in the evenings, while they told stories and tossed acorns? Would the ceramic discs that stored music on them still play? And the iceboxes where they kept wonderful frozen desserts stay cold?

Or would this artificial star—an unnatural body, created by the mouse king's greed and jealousy of the three queens—suck all those bits of magic back up to join the rest King Eiric had hoarded inside it?

"What would you do with the magic inside your artificial star, if we let you have the Celestial Fragments to bind it all up?" Witch-Hazel asked. She heard Fish-Breath draw a sharp breath behind her; she didn't know if he hoped she'd turn over the gems encrusting his body, or whether he had come to fear this mouse as quickly as she had.

"*Let* me?" the mouse king asked mockingly. His voice twisted like a knife. "As if you have the power to stop me. No one has the power to stop me. I drove your pathetic little party here, controlling my feline guards, chasing you down using their bodies as if they were extensions of my own. Cats who tower over me become mere puppets in my paws! I already have more magic in my star than you could ever imagine. The dribbles of magic you've played at wielding are nothing compared to the reservoir I've gathered here, impetuous squirrel, no matter how my queen-sisters may fear you."

"They don't fear me," Witch-Hazel countered. "Each one of them has invited me to join their realms, serving at their side."

"A way to control your power, because they feared it." The mouse king sneered. "Well, I don't need you, but I suppose I'd be willing to make the same offer—give back my Celestial Fragments, and you can serve at my side. As my marionette."

Witch-Hazel shuddered. The world was a madhouse mirror in this mouse's mind and words. The three queens didn't fear her. And she'd been to or at least seen all of their realms—there was dancing, feasting, growth, and joy. Here, there was nothing but shadows. There was nothing but the mouse king and the reflections he made of himself by usurping others. He used his portion of the magic in the world to control everyone and everything around him, delighting in turning entire people into nothing but puppets.

Witch-Hazel had heard stories—horror stories whispered by kits who should have been asleep in the dark of night—of a time, long ago, before the endless rivers had flowed between the earth and sky, before animals talked to each other at all, when squirrels and otters had been as silent as rocks and leaves. As wordless as the shadowcats under King Eiric's control.

Without magic flowing through the world, might animals lose the very spark of civilization? Would King Eiric even care if that happened? Was it his end goal? Nothing in the world to challenge him. Only him and his dragon's hoard of magic.

The Otter's Wings

And more than that—how could the mouse king claim his realm didn't have a celestial body of its own? *How dare he.*

Witch-Hazel felt the dirt under her paws, and now that she was sensitive to the flavor of magic, she felt the forces of magic sizzling through the earth, heavy and powerful. The whole planet was the Earthen Realm's celestial body.

And that should be enough.

For anyone.

The magic King Eiric had hoarded didn't belong to him. It belonged to the world.

"No," Witch-Hazel said. "You can't have the Celestial Fragments back. I found them. I gave them to my friend. And I will fight with every breath in my body, every whisper of blood through my veins, and all of the fire in my heart to stop you from taking them back."

As she mentioned each element and how it connected to her own body, Witch-Hazel felt an answering vibration in the dirt under her paws, as if the earth itself were listening to her, and promising to pass along her message—a cry for help and allyship—to her friends in the other realms. Because they were her friends.

She had raised Mercy from caterpillar to full grown god and travelled with Zwi until she'd found a home tree for her new hive. She'd returned Queen Amalah's treasure—lost and buried in a dead mole city—to her, and she'd helped Queen Kokeu to find denizens of her realm—zombies who'd been trapped between life and death—and return their souls to the endless party where they belonged.

All three of those queens had invited her to join their courts and become their closest courtier, not out of fear. Out of friendship. And it was time for Witch-Hazel to call on it.

Eiric had torn the pantheon of the gods in this world apart, creating competition where there should have been collusion; encouraging hoarding, when instead the wealth of magic could have been shared.

Witch-Hazel could do better.

And yet, as the answers came back to her, rolling like tiny earthquakes through the fabric of magic tying the universe together, they were frustratingly useless:

We cannot come to the Earthen Realm, spoke a voice like a crackling fire in Witch-Hazel's mind. *We support you,* whispered like a breeze through tall grasses. And finally, *we are watching and waiting,* bubbling like a brook over pebbles worn smooth by time.

The other queens wanted Witch-Hazel to win this fight, but they couldn't help her with it. The Earthen Realm had been warded against them, and only its ruler could invite them to enter.

So, all Witch-Hazel had to do was overthrow the mouse king and take down his magical wards. No problem. That's what Queen Kokeu had expected her to do anyway, right? Hadn't the cryptic koi told her: a crown already graced her head? All she had to do was take the crown from between the mouse king's round ears.

Witch-Hazel had never felt more supported—nor more alone—ever before. The weight of this fight fell squarely on her small shoulders.

"Come to me, dear otter," King Eiric said, gesturing with a miniscule paw. "Let me rid you of the burden you've been carrying in those useless rocks plaguing your natural body."

Fish-Breath, still clasping Witch-Hazel's paw, looked down at her, uncertain. The mouse king was offering him what he still wanted.

But Witch-Hazel shook her head. She saw out of the corner of her eye, the shadowcats advancing, surrounding them from all sides. "Fly us to the star!" she cried, throwing her free arm around Fish-Breath's waist, clinging tight to him.

He trusted her, and his wings flapped, lifting them from the ground and pulling them steadily higher. He wrapped his arms around her, so she could reposition herself more securely. They flew toward the star, and its light was overpowering.

"What now?" he asked, muzzle close to her pointed ears.

"The mouse king wants to use the Celestial Fragments like a knot, tying all the magic leaked from the Sun, Moon, and North Star into this new star forever. We need to use them like a conduit—letting the magic from this unnatural star flow back into the world."

"How?" Fish-Breath asked, flying in a curve around the star's side, orbiting it like a shooting star himself.

Witch-Hazel wasn't sure. "I ... I don't know. I can feel the magic flow through the Celestial Fragments." She'd called on it, drawing magic through those gemstones and into herself. "But what we need to do is free the magic trapped here; let it come flooding out of the star and into every corner of the world. All I know right now is I need to get closer to it."

A melodic voice surprised Witch-Hazel, and she looked over to see Dappled-Sun flying beside Fish-Breath. "The shadow passage that brought us here—" the bird sang. "Shadows are everywhere. Could you use those?"

"Maybe ..." Witch-Hazel's heart clenched, realizing all three of them had left Twiggy behind on the ground. A beaver engineer alone with a mad mouse king and his army of shadowcats. The mouse might be paw-sized to her, and the army only five strong ... but Witch-Hazel still didn't like those odds. Whatever she and Fish-Breath were doing, they needed to do it quickly, so they could get back to their friend. She had to untangle the magic inside the star. She could feel its threads, if she pulled on them just right ...

The Otter's Wings

"Fly into the star," Witch-Hazel said. She'd traversed the world's shadows like a spiderwebbed highway once now. She'd simply have to do it again, this time without the shadowcats to open the door, pointing the way. She'd pull the threads of magic along with her.

"Into the star?" Fish-Breath asked.

"Directly into it," she answered. Then craning her head to look at the songbird fluttering along beside them, she added, "And Dappled-Sun? Try to help Twiggy."

The flying otter and songbird had crested their orbit, reaching the perihelion of their flight at the top of the star. Dappled-Sun soared on, rounding the top so she could head back down to Twiggy on the ground below.

Fish-Breath, however, simply folded his wings against his back and dove. He crashed into the glimmering, shifting, glowing, glaring light of the star like an otter splashing into a sunbaked pond.

The light was warm and tingly all around them, like the feel of the magic flowing into Witch-Hazel through the conduits of the Celestial Fragments, except this wasn't a small sensation in her paws; it was a sensation filling her from the sharp tip of her claws to the sensitive ends of her whiskers. It felt too large for her corporeal body to hold. The magical light flowed through them as if their very bodies were as transparent to magic as glass was to light. Witch-Hazel felt insubstantial, like the mix of distant birdsong and sweet blackberry scent on the wind.

She felt like she could lose herself inside this star forever, wrapped in its warm tangled ribbons of magic. Let Fish-Breath bind the magic into itself with the Celestial Fragments, and the two of them would become one with it, simply another ebb and flow in its swirling eddies and currents. Lost, and yet more found than a simple creature like a squirrel can ever be unless a jovial otter sees her, knows her, and loves her back.

In the end, if Witch-Hazel had been the one wearing wings and encrusted with gems, all alone inside the star, she'd have lost herself there forever. King Eiric could have bound her inside and done what he wanted in the outside world. She wouldn't have cared, lost in the glowing dissolve of magic like a warm bath.

If Fish-Breath had been alone, he'd have been lost as well, unable to navigate the tangled ribbons of magic at all. But they were together, and Witch-Hazel remembered enough of being a squirrel in love with an otter to refuse to let herself dissipate like morning fog, burned away by the power of the star's magic into nothing more than an aspect of the star itself.

No, she reached out, and she found the other side of light. She reached for the darkness, and she found a way onto the network of shadows interwoven throughout every part of the world.

The magic followed her; a stream guided by her paw. It flowed into the shadows, gushing across the spiderweb of shadow highways like water breaking over a dam. Shadows existed in every corner of the world, and magic flowed into those corners, spreading out and soaking into the mundane world like raindrops absorbed into the grateful ground of a dry desert after a long awaited storm.

With all the magic gone, the star burst like a bubble. One moment perfect and glimmering; the next, as if it had never existed.

All the magic it had held returned to the world.

And Witch-Hazel was left, returned to her simple, corporeal form, held tightly in the arms of her otter. His wings flapped a final time and disappeared like a reflection on water when the angle changes.

Together, they floated down to the ground, Witch-Hazel controlling their fall with the remnants of the magic in the room, slipping through her paws like ropes she couldn't quite grip, sliding away before she could get ahold of them, but slowing and cushioning their fall before escaping her grasp.

Her paws touched the ground, and with a jolt, she felt the power of the earth answer to her. She had already won the fight. The mouse, Eiric, was no longer king here. There was no king.

Only a fourth queen.

Eiric squeaked his outrage and ordered the shadow-cats, "Attack this usurper!"

But without the light of the unnatural star shining down on them, bouncing and refracting off all of the glittering crystal facets in the cavern, the shadowcats were just cats. Tired looking tabbies, who glanced uncertainly at the miniscule mouse ordering them around, then at each other, and finally at Witch-Hazel.

One tabby lowered her head toward the ground, striking an elegant bow, and said, "My lady squirrel, Queen of the Earthen Realm, we are yours to command."

The other cats followed her lead, and then one by one, each of Witch-Hazel's friends bowed their heads as well. Her heart skipped, unsure of what to feel.

She wasn't different, not really. But her role had changed.

"What can we do for you first, my queen?" asked a second one of the cats.

"Bring me my crown," Witch-Hazel said, pointing at the furious mouse, squeaking and stomping, storming about like a tiny tempest in a single-serve teapot.

Without the power of the earth behind him, no matter how much trouble he'd caused before, he was just a mouse, and the cat easily lifted his golden crown from the top of his head.

Witch-Hazel's crown.

The mouse tried to grab the crown back, but another one of the cats lifted him easily in her paws and carried him away.

The squirrel lowered her own head to let the first cat place the crown upon it. Though, of course, she wouldn't have had to, as the cat stood nearly twice her height, like Fish-Breath and Twiggy. As the weight of the gold settled between her ears, the crown resizing itself to fit her perfectly, Witch-Hazel wondered if there should have been some kind of ceremony or ritual structure to the crowning of a new deity. But by the time the thought crossed her mind, it was already too late. She wore the crown of the Earthen Realm, just as Queen Kokeu had forecast she would.

The moment passed, simple and yet ceremonious in its own way. And Witch-Hazel found herself looking out at the cavern, filled with mice, moles, cats, and all kinds of creatures—all of the beings who had looked like nothing more than shadows while the unnatural star eclipsed them. These were her subjects, and they looked back at her expectantly.

Except for Fish-Breath. His muzzle had quirked into a lopsided smile, and he said, "Now you're the one encrusted with jewels."

"It's just a bit of gold," Twiggy said. "It doesn't change her any more than the Celestial Fragments changed you. She's still the same stubborn, difficult squirrel we've been following ever since she found us in the labyrinth, so many months ago. Just like you've been the same foolish, cheerful clown all along, beneath those wings which made you seem so dour."

Fish-Breath blinked and turned, craning his neck as if to look at his own back. He hadn't realized the wings were gone, and the biggest grin spread across his face when he discovered the truth of their absence. Then he held his paws up, checking them, and found them free of gems. He held them out toward Witch-Hazel and Twiggy, turning them palm up and then down, showing his friends the Moon Opal on his knuckle and Star Sliver in his wrist were really, finally gone.

Witch-Hazel took hold of his paws, needing to feel the change for herself, and as she ran her own paw pads over the places where the gems had been, she felt slight indentations under his thick fur. The Celestial Fragments' presence had changed him. But only a little.

"What do we do now?" Fish-Breath asked.

Twiggy gestured at the wooden ladders, walkways, and trellises laced around the edges of the cavernous geode, lit by flickering torches now that the room wasn't flooded with unnatural starlight, and said, "Have you ever seen such a rickety racket of structures? There are engineering feats in the tavern of Riverton that would put this whole place to shame. I have my work cut out for me, bringing the Earthen Realm into the modern age."

The cat who had crowned Witch-Hazel said, "The deposed king kept plans for all the contraptions and devices he intended to power with the star's magic once it was harnessed. We can show them to you."

"Yes, please!" Twiggy said. "That would be the perfect place to start."

Dappled-Sun came to land on her shoulder, and the cat led the two of them away. And like that, without having to say a single word, Witch-Hazel had a beaver seneschal to care for the practical side of the realm she'd overthrown, and that seneschal had a songbird assistant.

Witch-Hazel looked up at Fish-Breath and said, "Now, the earth is ours, and we make it into the world we want to live in."

"That sounds like fun," Fish-Breath said with a heart-melting grin. And reflected in his eyes, Witch-Hazel truly felt like a queen.

"It does, doesn't it?" she said.

There would be time to remove the wards that kept the queens from the other realms out of hers and invite them to a more ceremonial coronation later—possibly attended by Zwi and her honeybee daughters, and maybe even some of the mythical creatures Witch-Hazel had met during her travels—Mother the gryphon, Gloaming the unicorn, and the mysterious Leontaur. Those who had tricked her, confounded her, and tried to lead her astray would bow before her now.

There would be time for Witch-Hazel to test her magical powers, how they'd changed—diminished or grown—when the magic from the star had flowed outward, like a wave crashing against the world, spreading from a white-water crest into a thin wavelet. There would even be time to go back to Riverton, and maybe to check in on her squirrel family in the oak grove.

There would be time to see what changes magic had wrought on the world—what new flowers bloomed, how many more fairy rings of mushrooms sprouted, and what further wonders engineers like Twiggy could concoct. Perhaps the endless rivers would flow between the earth and sky again, or if not, perhaps Twiggy could build dirigibles to fly in their place.

They had time.

But for now, Witch-Hazel was with Fish-Breath, and that was enough. They could sing their own songs, dance their own dances, and let their hearts fly without the need of wings.

About the Author

Mary E. Lowd is a prolific science-fiction and furry writer in Oregon. She's had nearly 200 short stories and a dozen novels published, always with more on the way. Her work has won numerous awards, and she's been nominated for the Ursa Major Awards more than any other individual. She is also the founder and editor of Zooscape. Learn more at marylowd.com.

The Original
DUNGEON SOLITAIRE
Tomb of Four Kings

Still Available for Free

at

matthewlowes.com/games

Complete Rules
are Print-Ready and Playable
with any Standard Deck
of Playing Cards

Dungeon Solitaire
Labyrinth of Souls

TAROT CARD GAME

by Matthew Lowes
Illustrated by Josephe Vandel

Complete Rulebook
&
Labyrinth of Souls Tarot Deck
Available at
matthewlowes.com/games

Labyrinth of Souls Fiction

Fourteen books available!

For more information, visit
shadowspinnerspress.com

Made in the USA
Middletown, DE
20 October 2022